He never dreamed she was a virgin.

"Why didn't you say something?" he asked hoarsely.

"It doesn't matter."

"Yes, it does."

She shushed him by pressing a finger over his lips. "I know this is just for tonight. No commitments…"

"Why me?" he asked.

"Because I wanted you," she admitted with a sultry smile.

Bradford felt completely humbled by the fact that Rosanna had given herself to him. He buried his head against her neck, inhaled her essence. He never should have slept with her.

"Stop thinking," she said softly. "I needed you tonight. It's as simple as that."

"Nothing about this is simpl⸏⸏⸏⸏⸏⸏⸏⸏⸏⸏⸏ Still he didn't pull a⸏⸏⸏⸏⸏⸏⸏⸏⸏⸏⸏⸏⸏⸏⸏⸏ ⸏ad never been a ⸏⸏⸏⸏⸏⸏⸏⸏⸏⸏⸏⸏⸏ re of women and ⸏⸏⸏⸏⸏⸏⸏⸏⸏⸏⸏⸏⸏ ⸏e would be no dif⸏⸏⸏

Still, as he lower⸏⸏⸏⸏⸏⸏⸏⸏ ⸏uth and tasted her again, he knew he had to have her one more time. And then maybe another…

...way or release her, Bradford ha...
...noble man. He'd had his sha...
...never committed. And this on...
...ference.

...tered his mouth...

RITA HERRON

UP IN FLAMES

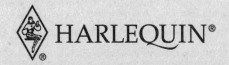
HARLEQUIN®

TORONTO • NEW YORK • LONDON
AMSTERDAM • PARIS • SYDNEY • HAMBURG
STOCKHOLM • ATHENS • TOKYO • MILAN • MADRID
PRAGUE • WARSAW • BUDAPEST • AUCKLAND

For all the fans who have kept my
NIGHTHAWK ISLAND series alive—
hope you like the firestarter twist!

ISBN-13: 978-0-373-88803-0
ISBN-10:   0-373-88803-1

UP IN FLAMES

Copyright © 2007 by Rita B. Herron

www.eHarlequin.com

Printed in U.S.A.

ABOUT THE AUTHOR

Award-winning author Rita Herron wrote her first book when she was twelve but didn't think real people grew up to be writers. Now she writes so she doesn't have to get a *real* job. A former kindergarten teacher and workshop leader, she traded her storytelling for kids for romance, and writes romantic comedies and romantic suspense. She lives in Georgia with her own romance hero and three kids. She loves to hear from readers, so please write her at P.O. Box 921225, Norcross, GA 30092-1225, or visit her Web site at www.ritaherron.com.

Books by Rita Herron

HARLEQUIN INTRIGUE
  755—UNDERCOVER AVENGER*
  790—MIDNIGHT DISCLOSURES*
  810—THE MAN FROM FALCON RIDGE
  861—MYSTERIOUS CIRCUMSTANCES*
  892—VOWS OF VENGEANCE*
  918—RETURN TO FALCON RIDGE
  939—LOOK-ALIKE*
  977—JUSTICE FOR A RANGER
1006—ANYTHING FOR HIS SON
1029—UP IN FLAMES*

*Nighthawk Island

CAST OF CHARACTERS

Detective Bradford Walsh—This jaded cop must stop a serial arsonist targeting Rosanna Redhill.

Rosanna Redhill—A woman plagued with special abilities—she fears they are evil and must keep them a secret.

Dr. Klondike—The doctor heading up the research experiment involving paranormal abilities. Is she hiding the identity of the firestarter because he is part of the project?

Dr. Salvadore—He's in charge of the subjects with the gift of telekinesis. Does he know more than he's telling about the firestarter?

Barry Coker—A convicted arsonist recently released on parole. Is he setting the fires in Savannah?

Manny Blunt—Famous for burning women who practiced witchcraft. Does he have a follower taking up where he left off?

Kevin Shaw—He claims he can freeze things with his hands, but is he lying about his power?

Louis Dunce—The secretive lab tech asked Rosanna on a date.

Johnny Walsh—Bradford put his little brother in jail for arson and murder. How far would Johnny go to get revenge on his brother?

Prologue

Four-year-old Rosanna Redhill gripped the charm around her neck as she huddled in the corner of her kitchen. Granny Redhill said the gris-gris would protect her.

She should have given her puppy, Little Doodlebug, one, too.

Her daddy was on a tear tonight. He'd been drinking that brown, smelly stuff. Cussing and pacing. Throwing things. He'd already broken an ashtray and a lamp.

And he'd kicked Little Doodlebug so hard that he wasn't moving.

She blotted at the tears on her face, and wished her mama was still here. But her mama had run away and hadn't come back.

Her daddy stumbled to the wooden table, grabbed his cigarettes and lit one. The smell made her stomach hurt.

"Rosanna! Come out, come out wherever you are."

She gulped and held her breath, hoping he wouldn't find her. But he knelt down and stabbed her with his beady eyes. Eyes that looked yellow and evil.

"Why are you hiding from Daddy?" he sneered.

She willed Doodlebug to get up and help her, but he didn't make a sound. Had her daddy killed him?

He reached for her, and she scrambled away and ran into the den. Wind rattled the windowpanes. The fire in the fireplace crackled and popped. Orange and red flames shot sparks into the dark room.

The big deer head on the wall glared down at her as if it was her fault he'd been shot. But her daddy had killed it, too.

She darted behind the big chair to hide. His feet pounded on the wood floor.

She closed her eyes, and in her mind saw Granny bent over her cauldron pot, the water boiling. Granny sprinkling in weird things like toad's feet, snakeskin and lizard's eyes. She could still smell the roots simmering. Hear Granny's soothing voice telling her stories about witches and voodoo. Rosanna wished she had a magic spell right now to save her from her daddy.

Something wet plopped on her head. She opened her eyes and looked up. The deer head was crying.

And her daddy was looming over her, his cheeks bulging red. He was mad as a hornet. And when daddy got mad…

She clenched her hands together. Prayed he'd go away. But his fingers clamped around her wrist. There was no place to hide.

Then she saw the firepoker leaning against the hearth. If she had it, she could swing it at him. She reached out her hand. Clawed for it.

But she was too far away.

A chant her granny used to say echoed in her head. She whispered it into the darkness.

Suddenly the poker flew off the hearth and slammed into her father's head. He bellowed and fell to his knees, blood dripping down his forehead.

"You're a devil just like your granny," he said. "I told your mama that. That's why she run off. She was scared of you." He staggered toward her. "Now, you're gonna be sorry."

He dug his fingernails into her skin, but a loud roar split the air. Then the deer head dropped from the wall and slammed against his skull.

A loud cracking, like the sound of thunder, followed, and she saw the bookcase falling. She screamed and jerked free just as it crashed down on top of her daddy's legs. He bellowed like a wild animal. Then his eyes rolled back in his head and he passed out.

She gulped back tears, saw the firepoker with blood on it and knew that she had caused it to move. Shaking all over, she laid her hand on the deer head. It was staring back at her, but it wasn't crying anymore.

It was smiling.

Chapter One

*Twenty-four years later, July 4—
Savannah, Georgia*

Detective Bradford Walsh was starving.
Starved for food.

Starved for a woman.

Starved for a reprieve from the sweltering
heat in Savannah, and a break from the
recent crime wave terrorizing the citizens.

But as he watched the blazing fire engulf-
ing Cozy's Café on River Street, the possibility of satisfying any of those hungers
that night quickly went up in smoke just like
the building had minutes ago.

Dammit. How long had it been since he'd
had a good meal? A decent night's sleep?

A night of hot sex?

A Fourth of July without trouble?

His partner, Parker Kilpatrick, joined him, soot darkening his jeans and shirt, sweat beading on his forehead. He and Parker had arrived first on the scene and had rushed in to make sure everyone escaped the blaze unharmed. In fact, his captain, Adam Black, knew about Bradford's history and had handpicked him to spearhead investigations into the recent arson crimes in the city.

Bradford was determined to prove that a screwup with his brother hadn't cost him his job.

Which was the only thing he had left since his family relationships disintegrated with his brother's arrest.

Dragging his mind back to the current situation, he assessed the scene. A half-dozen patrons milled around the edge of the sidewalk watching the building deconstruct. Thick plumes of gray smoke curled toward the sky, the orange, red and yellow flames shooting into the darkness. The owner, a pudgy Southern woman named Hazel, flapped her hands around, waving smoke away in between bouts of crying in her coffee-stained apron.

Bradford walked over to her and patted

her shoulder. "I'm sorry about your business, ma'am. But at least everyone escaped safely, and you can rebuild."

"We worked so hard to get this place going, to have a clean business. Then my husband died," she said between sobs. "I don't think I can start over by myself."

Compassion for the woman bled through Bradford. "How did the fire get started, ma'am? Was it in the kitchen?"

"No," she cried. "I was in the back, making my peach pies, when I heard someone shout that smoke was coming from the bathroom."

"All right, we'll check it out." He turned to his partner.

"This is the third fire in three weeks in the Savannah area," Parker said.

Bradford nodded. "Any signs of an accelerant?"

"No, but the fire chief just arrived. I'll make sure he checks for arson."

"Tell him to start in the men's room. Someone may have lit a match or dropped a cigarette in the trash." And paper towels would go up in seconds.

"It is a holiday," Parker said. "Maybe

some kids starting their fireworks a little early."

Bradford once again scanned the crowd. "Yeah, and the night is still young."

Parker strode toward the fire chief, and Bradford mentally ticked over the facts they had so far on all three fires. The first one was set at a cottage on Tybee Island not far from the one he was renting, and appeared to be accidental, a fluke with old wiring. The second, an abandoned warehouse on the outskirts of town had aroused questions, but there had been no evidence of accelerant present. The firemen had speculated that a homeless person staying inside might have dropped a cigarette butt, and with old paint thinner stored inside, the building had caught fire.

This one—smoke in the bathroom, not the kitchen—could have been accidental, but on the heels of the others, it definitely struck a chord of suspicion.

Could there be a connection?

He scanned the spectators who'd gathered to gawk. An elderly couple walking their Yorkie had stopped to console a young mother. Three teenage girls wearing short shorts huddled next to a couple of gangly boys taking pictures with their cell phones. A teenage prank? No, they looked curious, but not like arsonists or vandals.

Two men in suits stood chatting quietly. A gaggle of tourists with cameras and souvenirs from the gift shops on River Street hovered around, enraptured by the blaze, but no one stuck out as suspicious looking.

The hairs on the back of his neck prickled. An older black woman in voodoo priestess garb watched, her colorful clothing highlighted by the firelight. Beside her stood a nondescript blond man in his early twenties.

A movement to the left caught Bradford's attention, and he spotted a woman with flaming-red curly hair. She was slender, wore a long, flowing skirt, peasant blouse and beads around her neck. A short brunette leaned near her and said something, but they were out of earshot.

Although the redhead looked like some kind of throwback to the seventies, his gaze met hers, and something hot and instant flared inside him. She was so natural, so earthy and untamed-looking, that his baser primal side reacted immediately. Her eyes were the palest green he'd ever seen, and looked almost translucent. For a moment, he felt as if she'd cast some kind of spell on him.

Then she darted away, through the maze of onlookers as if she'd sensed the connection and couldn't get away from him fast enough.

He started to follow her. But heat scalded his neck, wood crackled and the sound of walls crashing shattered the hushed silence. The owner of the café cried out, other onlookers shrieked and he halted. He couldn't go chasing some woman during an investigation, not unless he thought she was a suspect. And he had no reason to think that.

After all, ninety percent of firestarters were men, not women. Bradford had studied the profiles. A large percentage were out to collect insurance money or exact revenge. But there was another percent that had a fixation. To them fire was a living, breathing monster. The obsessive compulsion to watch something burn escalated with each fire set.

He knew because his little brother had been one of them.

Shaking off the troubling memories of his past, he squared his shoulders. If an arsonist was playing havoc in Savannah, Bradford damn well wouldn't rest until he found the son of a bitch and put him behind bars.

FINGERS OF TENSION crawled along Rosanna Redhill's nerve endings as she passed the graveyard with its tombs and granite markers standing at attention, honoring those who'd passed to the other side. Death surrounded her, as did the stories of witches, voodoo and sin in the city.

Smoke painted the sky in a hazy gray, floating across the tops of the graves like ghosts whispering to the heavens. The pungent smell of the blazing building followed her, chasing away the lingering scent of the therapeutic herbs and candles in her gift shop, Mystique.

At least no one had died in the fire.

Still, the blaze left her with the oddest feeling that something supernatural was happening in Savannah. That something dangerous and evil was lurking nearby. That someone in the crowd was not quite normal.

Like her.

But it was that cop who had her rattled so badly that she was trembling as she rushed toward the apartment she'd rented in one of the Victorian row houses. Her friend Natalie, a girl she'd met at the Coastal Island Research Park, CIRP, three months ago, hurried along beside her.

"Why did you run, Rosanna?" Natalie asked.

She darted up the sidewalk and onto the porch, then jammed her key toward the keyhole in her apartment door. Her fingers shook, though, and she dropped the key, then had to bend to retrieve it and start all over.

How could she explain without revealing the truth about her childhood? Without divulging her secrets? Secrets she'd guarded over for the past twenty-four years.

"Rosanna?" Natalie said softly. "Come on, tell me what's wrong? You looked spooked back there."

Rosanna pivoted, wondering if her new friend had a sixth sense. The experiment she'd joined at the Coastal Island Research Park involved testing for special abilities. Some of the participants were control subjects; others claimed to have various gifts ranging from telekinesis to psychic powers to those who communed with the dead. They were beginning a support group session this week, but so far no one had been forced to share his or her reason for being involved in the study.

"I don't like cops," Rosanna said, admitting the partial truth. "They make me nervous."

Natalie arched a dark brow. "Hmm. I thought those two at the scene of the fire were kind of cute."

Cute was not a word Rosanna would have attached to the hulking male cop who'd stared at her through the crowd. He was tall, broad-shouldered like a linebacker, with a square jaw, strong nose, cleft chin and thick hair as black as the soot from the embers of the charred wood. Even his eyebrows were thick and powerful looking, framing his eyes in a way that emphasized his coldness.

He had a dark side. Whether it was anger, his job, or the criminals he'd dealt with, something had hardened him.

Still, for a minute when he'd looked at her, she'd felt some cosmic force draw her to him.

The reason she'd run. The last person she'd ever get involved with was a cop.

Rosanna pushed open the door and hurried into the foyer, trying to shake the cobwebs of lust from her brain.

After her father had died, she'd been sent to live with her grandmother, a descendant of a witchdoctor. Rosanna had grown up a recluse with Granny Redhill, shunned by some, yet welcomed by the underground population of Savannah's believers in the supernatural.

She had never had a boyfriend. Had never wanted a man before. And it had never bothered her that she was alone. She *liked* being alone.

So why had she been drawn to that detective?

"Earth to Rosanna?" Natalie said with a laugh. "What are you thinking?"

"About that fire," Rosanna said. "There were two others in the past few weeks."

"But they weren't related," Natalie said. "Besides, it's been so dry with this heat wave that fires have been breaking out all across the South."

True. So why was she nervous?

"Come on, Rosanna, let's go to the Pink

Martini. They have live music on Saturday nights. Maybe we'll meet some guys."

Rosanna sighed and dropped her purse onto the ottoman in the den. She'd read her own tarot cards, and a lovelife was not in her future. "You go ahead, Nat. I'll just curl up with a good book tonight and go to bed early."

"No," Natalie protested. "It's the Fourth of July celebration. Don't you want to see the fireworks?"

"We just saw enough fireworks for me," Rosanna said.

Natalie pushed her toward her bedroom. "Not for me. I've been begging you for weeks to party with me, and I'm not taking no for an answer. Now go put on something sexy."

Rosanna glanced down at her colorful skirt and sandals. She liked her gypsy look. "I don't exactly have good luck in the relationship department." Because she could never be her true self. Her own parents had thought she was a devil child and hadn't been able to love her. And she'd proven her father right that fatal day…

"Please," Natalie said, giving her another

push. "It's not safe to go barhopping alone. I need a buddy."

Her last words convinced Rosanna. With the recent crime wave in town, Natalie was right. Rosanna didn't have very many friends. She didn't want to lose this one.

In her bedroom, she slipped on a black sundress, strappy silver sandals and silver hoop earrings. Nothing she could do with her mop of hair, so she left it loose, then added some lip gloss. Seconds later, she and Natalie headed back outside into the hot, sultry summer air.

But once again, a chill of foreboding tiptoed up her spine as they strolled toward River Street.

She spun around twice to see if someone was following her, but saw nothing. Still, tension charged the air, and she sensed something dark and sinister in the shadows.

HE STILL FELT the heat of the flames from the café burning his hands, singeing his hair, the smoke filling his lungs. And he tasted the *fear*.

Laughter bubbled in his chest. The terrified screams of the onlookers was music to his ears. Food for his hungry heart.

While the firefighter raced to extinguish his handiwork, he had stood in the shadows of the live oaks, letting the spidery web of Spanish moss shroud him. His heart raced, his blood hot from the excitement of watching the flames light up the inky sky and the knowledge that he had exerted control over all of them.

They would never catch him because he had left no evidence behind. Laughter bubbled in his throat. Detective Bradford Walsh would spin in circles.

Perfect. He hated Bradford Walsh.

Now the woman was a different story. He'd felt her presence, sensed that she was like him. Different.

What her talents were he didn't know. But he would find out.

And he would use her if needed.

He followed her now. Had seen her before, but couldn't place where.

She was dressed to kill and heading toward the party end of town. Probably on the prowl for a man to fulfill her fantasies.

He had fantasies of his own.

His thirst for another fire already burned inside him, stronger and more intense than before. The city would host a fireworks show in the park tonight, but those would be pitiful compared to his work.

The café fire was only the beginning of the festivities he had planned.

But he had cut short his fun in watching the flames die down at the café because of this *woman*. He wanted that lost time back, those lost moments of joy, of seeing the final embers dwindle to ashes. That part usually satisfied and fed him for hours. Sometimes days. But not tonight.

She had robbed him of that pleasure.

And she would suffer.

In fact, he just might set her afire and watch her skin erupt into flames like kindling.

Chapter Two

Bradford spent the next two hours interviewing the witnesses from the café fire.

Frustration gnawed at him. No one stuck out as a possible arsonist. No one had seen or heard anything suspicious.

Of course, the holiday crowds and tourist season made it easy for a culprit to hide. Restaurants and bars overflowed, catering to the party scene. A ship of sailors had docked and they were combing the streets on their furlough.

If the guy was among them or the tourists, he could disappear tomorrow.

Families had gathered in the squares for picnics and special booths had been set up for the holiday offering cotton candy, sno cones, frozen lemonade and other treats. Face-painting, tarot card readers, clowns, balloon artists and mimes entertained in the square, and a vendor sold voodoo dolls to passersby. The ever-present ghost tours strolled along the graveyards and historic district adding to the atmosphere.

Still, excitement sizzled in the balmy summer air, the sound of children and partiers filling the streets growing louder in anticipation of the upcoming fireworks show.

Hazel's son Robby had arrived and tried to console his mother while Parker interviewed her.

Bradford listened, then cornered Chief Jackson as the last of the flames died down. Now the ruins, soaked with water, looked like a sludgy mess of charred wood and plastic.

"What do you think?" Bradford asked.

"It's too early to tell," Chief Jackson said. "We'll have to sift through the debris, take samples, run tests…" The tall African-American man shifted, restless himself. "Did you learn anything from the interviews?"

"Afraid not. But three fires in three weeks. Not all accidental."

"I'll review the other two scenes," Jackson said. "See if my men missed anything. Look for a connection."

Bradford nodded. He'd already talked to the officers himself. In the first two instances, the sites had been vacant. At this one there were people inside. Which meant, if the incidents were related, their perpetrator was taking more chances, growing more confident, more aggressive.

And that he'd just begun his reign of terror. Next time, there might be casualties.

They had to stop him before that happened.

SOMEONE WAS WATCHING her.

Rosanna pivoted in the dark corner of the bar, searching the faces, hunting for someone familiar, or maybe a stranger staring at her. But no one stood out.

Shivering in spite of the heat, she tried to convince herself that the fire and then walking by the graveyard had made her paranoid. After all, for years after her father's death, she'd had nightmares that he might claw his way from his coffin and try to drag her into hell with him. The fire tonight had reminded her of that nightmare.

The image of that cop helping the café owner to safety returned. He'd been kind and gentle and had consoled the older woman as if he cared.

But when he'd looked at her, she'd seen a coldness that chilled her to the bone.

Determined to put him out of her mind, she studied the dance floor. White lights glittered and popped intermittently across the room, an indoor fireworks show and hopping singles scene. Not one she was accustomed to being a part of.

She sipped a Lemon Drop martini while she watched the hump-and-grind show on the dance floor. Bodies gyrated, sliding against other bodies, men wrapped around women, skin to skin, a game of foreplay in public that made her body tighten with need.

And resurrected images of that detective again.

For a brief second, she pictured the two of them swaying to the music, his big, muscled arms holding her tight, his thigh slipping between her heat, his thick lips skating over hers. Desire shot through her.

A good-looking, blond architect paired up with Natalie and they headed to the dance floor. During the next half hour, Rosanna fended off unwanted advances.

Now she remembered the reason she avoided the clubbing scene.

She'd been alone all her life. And she didn't mind it. No one to worry about. No one to pry into her secrets.

No one to find out about her past.

And no one pawing at her.

A balding guy wearing a skeleton T-shirt and holey jeans sauntered toward her with a beer in hand. "Wanna dance, baby?"

She gritted her teeth, wondering why she attracted the weirdos. Maybe because she was eccentric herself?

"No, thanks."

He frowned and cut his eyes over her as if she'd angered him. Uncomfortable with his reaction, she slid off the stool and headed to the ladies' room. She sensed him following, but refused to turn around.

Near the ladies' room, another man at the bar made eye contact with her. He was tall, wore a black silk shirt and black dress pants. But instead of approaching her, he removed a lighter, flicked it open and pressed the starter until a small golden flame shot up. Then a slow smile crept over his face.

A smile that did not quite reach his eyes, one that sent a ripple of tension through her.

Anxious to escape his scrutiny, she ducked into the ladies' room. The line snaked through the cramped bathroom, and it took several minutes to reach a stall. Just as she closed the door, a loud explosion rocked through the room.

Screams filled the air, the sound of panicked scuffling following. She tried to jerk open the door but it was stuck, so she dropped to her knees to look under the stall. Smoke curled through the room and another explosion rocked the floor. Splintered wood crashed from the ceiling, pelting her, and the smoke thickened. She scrambled beneath the opening, pushed to her feet and ran for the door, but when she opened it, a wooden beam crashed down and flames exploded, blocking her exit.

In the bar, chaos had broken out. Flames shot upward, eating the wood and hissing as it danced through the room. People screamed and stampeded to the exit, debris rained down, and bar glasses shattered and spewed glass in all directions. She spotted a couple of people on the floor, blood flowing from one man's head. Then she saw Natalie trapped beneath a gigantic light fixture.

Oh God, no…she wasn't moving. She had to get to her friend, save her.

But heat seared her and crackling wood popped near her feet. There was no other way to get out of the bathroom. No window. No back exit.

She was trapped with the flames growing higher all around her.

THE SCENT OF SMOKE and singed fabric permeated Bradford's clothes as he and Parker left the Savannah square and maneuvered through the crowded streets.

The fireworks were in full swing, but he wanted to go back to the little house he'd rented on Tybee Island, wolf down a pizza and crash.

Parker leaned back in the seat, whistling a blues tune beneath his breath, looking relaxed now that the café excitement had ended. But Bradford's body felt wired, jittery, as if he was waiting on the other ball to drop. He'd had these same antsy feelings in the military on missions, on missing persons cases in Atlanta. The night his father had died.

The night he'd discovered the extent of his brother's problems.

The traffic came to a congested halt, and he veered down a side street where two restaurants and a new bar had opened up, then cursed.

Ahead he spotted trouble. More smoke curling toward the sky. Flames shooting from the roof of the Pink Martini.

"Hell, do you see that?" Parker pointed to the nightclub.

"Yeah, call it in." While Parker called dispatch, Bradford flipped on the siren, gunned the engine and screeched around an illegally parked car. In seconds, both he and Parker jumped out and ran toward the building.

"Fire trucks are on their way!" Parker shouted.

Bradford scanned the street where a panicked mob poured onto the sidewalks. People raced toward cars, the downtown area, some running as if the flames might chase them down, others huddling in shock and hysteria.

"Let's see if everyone got out!" Bradford shouted over the confusion.

As soon as they entered the bar, Bradford assessed the situation. This fire was ten times worse than the one at the café, and already engulfed half the room. Although the emergency sprinklers had kicked in, the thin jets of water weren't enough to douse the overpowering blaze, which was feeding greedily on the alcohol. Wood, glass, tables, drinks, lighting equipment—everything lay in shambles.

What the hell had happened here? How had the fire spread so rapidly?

He cut his eyes through the haze, searching for victims, someone trapped, hurt, needing assistance. The fire was a monster, the gray smoke so thick he could barely see, so he removed a handkerchief and covered his mouth. Somewhere amidst the crackling timber and the haze of shattering glass he heard a scream.

"My God," Parker muttered. "There's a woman trapped over there. I'm going after her!"

"I heard someone else in the back," Bradford yelled. "I'm going to check."

Without waiting for a response, he darted

through the patches of flames, coughing into the handkerchief, searching through the thick plumes of smoke.

A curly haired young man wearing an apron who must have been a server lay face-down on the floor, arms and legs sprawled at awkward angles. Bradford knelt and checked for a pulse, but he couldn't find one. Dammit.

Then he saw the blood pooling beneath the man's face and neck. Bradford lifted his head slightly, and grimaced. A huge chunk of glass had pierced the man's throat. Another was embedded in one eyeball.

It was too late for the poor guy. He was already dead.

A terrified scream pierced the air again, faint and hoarse, barely discernible over the roar of the flames.

Heat seared his back, face and hands, but he forged on toward the back.

"Help me!"

His lungs and throat burned as he spotted the caller. A woman lay on the floor, trapped by a wooden beam. She was using her bare hand to beat away the flames crawling toward her skirt. Another burning beam lay behind her.

He raced to her, jerked off his shirt and swatted the flames.

"Help me!" she cried again. "I have to save my friend."

He glanced at her face and recognized her immediately. The redhead he'd seen in the crowd outside Cozy's.

"Please," she whispered. "I have to find Natalie."

She broke into a coughing fit, and he handed her his handkerchief, then stood and dragged the beam off her legs. She tried to stand, but stumbled, so he swooped her up in his arms and ran toward the front door, praying they made it out in time before the monster eating the building swallowed them completely.

Chapter Three

Rosanna coughed, clinging to her rescuer as he hauled her into his arms. The last few terrifying minutes rushed back, fear tightening her lungs.

She'd been trapped in the bathroom. No way out. But she refused to give up. She had to get to Natalie.

She'd splashed water from the bathroom sink on her clothes hoping they wouldn't catch fire when she ran through the spiking flames in the doorway. But another beam had fallen and she'd collapsed as it slammed down onto her legs.

Her ankle throbbed, her throat ached and she felt dizzy. She squinted through the smoke, though, desperately searching for her friend. Maybe she'd escaped. Maybe she was huddled in the mob pouring onto the streets.

A siren wailed. Then another. Police cars, ambulances and two fire trucks screeched through the mass, all arriving at once and jumping into motion.

"Miss, are you all right?" a gruff voice asked.

She tried to answer, but her voice squeaked out, low and pain-filled. Disoriented, she blinked through the darkness, but the raging fire illuminated her rescuer's face, and her stomach tightened. He was the detective she'd seen questioning spectators at Cozy's earlier. He had saved Hazel, and now her.

She clutched his open shirt in a death grip as he dodged the flames and falling debris. Outside, she dragged in gulping breaths of fresh air, then swallowed against the dryness in her throat, aware of his masculinity and the power of his body as he carried her toward the ambulance.

Her body glided downward, scraping over the detective's massive thighs as he lowered her onto the stretcher. For a brief second, he pushed errant strands of her hair from her forehead. The gesture was so tender and gentle that tears pricked her eyes.

"Miss, are you okay?"

She nodded. "My friend…" she whispered. "Natalie Gorman, she fell. Find her, see if she's all right."

He nodded and squeezed her arm. "I will. What does she look like? What's she wearing?"

"Brown hair, a green dress!"

An EMT met them and shoved an oxygen mask toward her.

"Check her out!" The detective shouted, then he raced back toward the burning building.

The EMT examined her hands and arms for burns. They tingled from the heat, but she'd survived without any major injuries. "Are you hurt anywhere?"

Rosanna tried to tell him that she was okay, but again she broke out in a coughing fit.

The weighty pull of the smoke and exhaustion pulled her under, and she drifted into unconsciousness.

BRADFORD DARTED back toward the blazing building searching for his partner, but he didn't see him anywhere.

Two pairs of officers had arrived on the scene, and were trying to manage traffic and contain the crowd. He quickly explained what had happened and asked them to canvas the people who'd been inside, as well as the spectators on the street for information.

"See if you can find a Natalie Gorman, too," he said. "Her friend was asking about her. Brown hair. Green dress."

He pushed his way back through the mob, but didn't see a brown-haired woman in a green dress. And no Parker. He radioed him, but Parker didn't respond, and panic seized Bradford.

He headed to the front door to go back inside, but a fireman grabbed him. "You can't go in. Too dangerous."

"Detective Walsh, SPD." He flashed his badge. "My partner may still be inside. And another woman."

The burly man's expression clearly looked doubtful that they'd find anyone still alive. But he turned to one of the other rescue workers. "Search for survivors."

Bradford paced the sidewalk feeling helpless and angry. He should be questioning people, hunting for clues as to how the fire started, but fear kept him watching the doorway, listening.

Finally one of the rescue workers appeared, sweating and cursing. "We have a live one, trapped. Need equipment." He grabbed an ax from the truck.

"Let me help," Bradford pleaded.

The burly man put a hand to Bradford's chest as his coworker ran back inside. "No, stay put. You do your job, we'll do ours."

Bradford scraped sweaty hair from his forehead as another firefighter grabbed an ax and followed his coworker inside the blaze.

Heat scalded Bradford's face and a wave of anger crashed over him a second later when one of the men carried an unconscious woman outside. He ran to check on her, but the firefighter shook his head. "She's dead," he said. "Looks like she took a blow to the head."

Bradford saw her blood-soaked hair, the green dress, and grimaced. Then he noticed the tiny purse with the strap still wrapped around her wrist. He unsnapped the bag, checked her ID, then muttered a curse.

Natalie Gorman. The redhead's friend.

God, he'd have to tell her.

"Your buddy tried to save her, but a wall crashed on him," the firemen said. "We'll have him out in a minute."

Suddenly two rescue workers rushed out, yelling for the paramedics who met them with a stretcher. "He's alive, but we've got injuries. Multiple contusions to the body, second- and third-degree burns, his leg needs to be set…"

Bradford shouldered his way to the ambulance, his chest clenching when he saw Parker's limp body. He was unconscious; nasty blisters were already forming on his charred arms and hands. His leg looked twisted and mangled below the knee, his color ashen.

The EMT's secured his head and neck, started oxygen and an IV drip, and quickly loaded him in the ambulance.

"Is he going to make it?" Bradford asked.

The EMT shrugged. "We can't say yet. We need to get him to the hospital ASAP. What's his name?"

"Parker Kilpatrick," Bradford said. "He's a detective with the SPD."

"Is he allergic to anything?" one of the EMT's asked.

"No."

A frown marred the second EMT's face. "If you know his family, contact them."

"He doesn't have any family," Bradford said grimly.

The medic closed the doors, the siren began to screech, and the ambulance rolled away, the lights twirling.

NIGHTMARES OF FIRE, death, hell and eternal damnation consumed Rosanna. She struggled against the exhaustion, but lost the battle and closed her eyes. She was suffocating, couldn't breathe. The fire engulfed her hair and body, and her skin sizzled. Then her father's nasty smile found her as he climbed from the grave and grabbed her.

Then she was in the bar. Beside her, a man lay on the floor, his eyes wide pools of nothing, blood floating around his head like a red river. Her friend was sprawled face-down with fire shooting sparks around her, chewing at her hair and fingers. Rosanna's own skin burned, was frying, sliding off bone until black, sooty ashes fell like brittle, dead leaves onto the sodden floor.

She jerked awake for the hundredth time, and searched the sterile hospital room, wishing she were home in her own bed, wishing she'd talked Natalie out of going to the Pink Martini. Wishing she had someone to talk to, someone who cared that she was lying here alone, dirty and scared.

A knock sounded at the door. Quiet. Barely discernible. The doctor, most likely.

"Come in," she said in a hoarse voice.

The door squeaked open, and the detective who'd rescued her stuck his face through the opening. His thick, wavy black hair was ruffled, looked as if he'd jammed his hands through it a dozen times, and soot and exhaustion colored his face. "Are you awake, miss?"

"Yes, please, come in…"

His boots pounded on the floor as he strode toward her. Did he have news about Natalie?

One look into his troubled, dark eyes and she knew the answer before she even asked him.

"My name is Detective Bradford Walsh."

"Rosanna Redhill," she whispered. "Thank you for saving me."

He shrugged, but his jaw remained rigid as if he didn't want or expect her gratitude. "How are you feeling?"

His rough, thick voice skated over raw nerve endings.

"I'm fine." She clutched the sheets between shaking fingers, praying she was wrong about the bad news. "Did you find Natalie?"

He nodded, stepped toward her. Shadows haunted his eyes, eyes that had seen violence and death and sorrow.

"I'm so sorry. My partner tried to save her…."

"Oh God, no…" Her voice broke, and she curled into a ball, and pressed her fist to her mouth to stifle a sob.

He lowered himself onto the bed, gently stroked the hair from her face, then wiped a tear trickling down her cheek.

"How?" she asked in a tortured whisper.

"A head injury. The firefighter managed to get her out before the flames reached her."

Thank God. She couldn't stand that image in her head. Still, grief swelled in her chest.

She sucked in a sharp breath, determined to hold herself together until he left, but another sob escaped her, and he pulled her into his arms and held her. The gesture was so kind that it undid her, and she clutched him, not wanting to let go. For the first time in her life, she didn't want to be alone.

Poor Natalie. She had been so young and vivacious, so full of life with so much ahead of her. Her new apartment, internship, classes at the College of Art & Design…

He stroked her hair again, and she gulped back more tears, the tension in his hard body reminding her that he was only a stranger being kind, not a real friend. She couldn't lean on him….

Finally she swiped at her eyes, managed to regain control. "What about your partner? Is he okay?"

He cleared his throat, then glanced down at his hands. "Parker is alive, but in critical condition. He suffered burns and multiple wounds. His leg was crushed and his lung collapsed."

With an anguished look on his face, he pulled away and stood, putting distance between them. Guilt tightened her throat and chest. Why had she survived and Natalie died? Why had his friend suffered?

"I'd like to ask you some questions about the fire…if you're up for it."

She drew her knees up and wrapped her arms around them. "I don't know what I can tell you. I went to the ladies' room, then I heard something crash and I heard screaming. People panicked and ran out."

"You don't know how the fire started?"

She shook her head. "The stall door was stuck, so I had to crawl underneath it. By the time I reached the door to the bar, a beam had fallen, and flames filled the doorway blocking my path." She hesitated, felt those moments of panic and fear clawing at her. Saw the fire chewing at her legs when she'd fallen. Heard that second beam come roaring down on her. Her own scream of helpless terror.

She'd thought she was going to die. Had tried to push the beam off of her, first with her hands, then her mind, but there had been no time.

"Did you see anyone suspicious before then?" he asked.

"I…don't think so." Her head felt fuzzy,

disoriented again, and she closed her eyes, tried to concentrate, but all she could do was think about Natalie screaming. Natalie dying. Natalie never coming back.

"You were at the café earlier tonight, too, weren't you?"

She clenched her hands, forced her eyes back open. "Yes, I can't believe it. Two fires in one night."

He frowned. "You were inside when the fire broke out?"

She nodded reluctantly.

"Why did you run away?" he asked, his voice harder now. "We were questioning everyone at the scene."

She couldn't quite look at him. "I don't know. I was upset. I just wanted to escape."

"Did you see anything suspicious inside the café?"

"No."

He studied her for a long moment, and she willed him to leave, not to push her anymore. Her head ached, her eyes hurt and grief for Natalie clogged her throat.

"I'll let you rest," he said gruffly. "But I'll be back tomorrow when you're feeling better."

She nodded, miserable, still shaking uncontrollably. She wanted to curl up and cry for her friend, wanted to be alone in her sorrow.

Yet she didn't want him to go. Didn't want to be alone. She'd been alone all her life.

But he stepped out the door and closed it behind him, leaving her with her misery and the memory of her friend's face to haunt her.

His question echoed in her head. Had she seen anyone suspicious at the café or the bar? Had someone set that fire intentionally?

If so, then he had murdered Natalie...

HIS BODY SWELLED with arousal as he lingered in the shadows across from the Pink Martini. So much chaos. People panicking. Crying. Screaming. Gawking in horror and awe at the amazing fireworks display he'd started.

The firefighters had worked so diligently, sweating and shouting orders, hacking away fallen debris to save the injured and extinguish the mountainous blaze. They'd done their best to drown out his handiwork, but they had been too late. Too late to save the woman and man who'd died.

Death…such a nice perfect ending to a dull day. Except neither had actually melted into the fire because their bodies had been rescued first.

Adrenaline fired his blood at the thought of watching flesh and skin sizzle, and he realized that the high from watching wood and plastic burn was no longer enough to satisfy him.

He wanted, needed more. Craved the deeper, more exhilarating euphoria arousing him now at the thought of a body being consumed by the flames.

Yes, next he wanted to see a human burn.

Maybe the redhead…

Her hair was the same rich red, orange and yellow of the flames. He was drawn to her. Wanted to touch her. Make her quiver with fear. Elicit a scream from her pale throat as he turned her body into a playground for his pleasure.

He had seen the terror in her eyes when she'd been trapped in that bathroom. But she had shown amazing courage by running through the blaze.

Then she'd gone down, and a surge of excitement had seized him. She had been trapped beneath the fiery beam of wood. The fire would have eaten her alive in seconds.

Had it not been for that cop. The one man he hated.

It was the second time tonight Bradford Walsh had shown up and ruined *his* fun. Pretending to be some kind of savior…

But *he* knew the real detective Walsh— Brad boy he liked to call him.

Brad boy, the traitor.

Soon everyone else would see him for the weak failure he was.

A chuckle rumbled from his chest. Brad boy had no idea who he was dealing with. Or the power *he* possessed.

He had the gift of fire in his fingers. He would use it again and again, make each mark more impressive.

And no one could stop him.

Chapter Four

Rosanna Redhill's tortured, tearstained face haunted Bradford as he drove back to the bar. The firefighters were still battling the remnants of the blaze, the arson investigator from the county surveying the scene.

He strode toward Adam Black, the captain of the department.

"How's Kilpatrick?" Black asked.

Bradford shook his head. "Alive, but critical. Burns, a crushed leg and lung."

Black frowned, anger darkening his eyes. "How about you?"

"Pissed." Bradford gestured toward the ashes and embers of the bar, then around at the crowd still watching. "This one can't be accidental."

"I agree, that's why I called the CSI team out here immediately. I think we're dealing with a serial arsonist. And he just upped the stakes."

Bradford nodded in agreement. So far, he liked Captain Black. He was fair, smart, commanded respect and knew the inner-workings of Savannah and the Coastal Island Research Park. "You're right. And he's going down for murder," Bradford said, thinking about Rosanna's friend Natalie.

"You're done tonight. Go home, get some rest," Black ordered.

"No, I want to help here. I have to."

Ignoring Black's scowl, he joined the other officers questioning the spectators, and spent the next two hours trying to get a lead on what had happened. But everyone he questioned shared the same story. They hadn't seen anyone set the fire. Flames had suddenly shot up from behind the bar. Then near the doorway, and on the stage.

Possibly faulty lighting? He didn't think so. Someone had set the fire; he just had to figure out who and how they'd done it.

The owner of the bar, a big guy named Benny, looked shaken and furious. "I can't believe this damn mess. I just opened the bar this month."

Like Hazel, the man had invested all his money into the establishment. He was insured, but the labor costs and time spent rebuilding would mean more money lost.

If Benny had intentionally set the fire for insurance purposes, why do so when the bar was filled to capacity? He would have waited until it was empty, wouldn't have chanced injuries or deaths, which would stir more questions and bring more serious charges against him if caught.

Two hours later, Black informed him that they had everyone's contact information and again ordered him to go home. They would meet in the morning with the CSI team, then officers would be dispersed to requestion the people who'd been in the bar.

Exhausted, the adrenaline and anger that had fueled Bradford to keep working waned as he drove toward Tybee Island.

He'd thought living near the ocean might provide a few days of relaxation in between shifts. That the sea air and warm weather might improve his mood swings and help him regain his control over a temper that had nearly cost him his job back in Atlanta.

But so far he'd yet to have a day off to enjoy the beach or to go fishing.

As he left town, the city gave way to narrow country roads sprinkled with sea oats and small weathered shacks and cottages. He crossed the bridge and inhaled the salt air and smell of the marshland.

Though the island was only a few miles from downtown Savannah, the celebration had drawn a large crowd. Traffic was a bitch, and it took him over thirty minutes to reach the small house he'd rented. He killed the engine, climbed out and walked up the shell-lined driveway.

Wiping sweat from his brow with the back of his arm, he unlocked the door, flipped on a light and welcomed the churning sound of the air conditioner. A frozen pizza, a shower and some shut-eye before the next shift would rejuvenate him.

He only hoped the holiday didn't bring out more crazies tonight. After all, it was a full moon. And celebrations meant boozing, which often led to trouble.

His own past proved that to be a fact. His little brother, Johnny…

A drunk. An arsonist. A murderer.

In jail now.

And he hated Bradford for it. Blamed him for everything. His screwups. His father's death.

His arrest and sentencing.

One reason Bradford had relocated after leaving Atlanta. That and the need for a detective here in Savannah.

He'd thought he'd seen it all over his years, had worked special ops in the marines, had been assigned to a missing persons unit in Atlanta, but the bizarre cases with CIRP and Nighthawk Island topped the list of stranger-than-fiction and had piqued his interest.

Tonight's fires had nothing to do with that, though. But they did make him wonder.

He heated up the pizza, grabbed a beer from the fridge, then took them outside on the patio to eat. The earthy smell of grass, ocean and sea oats helped to cleanse his lungs of the smoke, but the images in his mind refused to disappear.

The blazing building. The dead man on the floor with his jugular sliced. The pale face of Natalie Gorman in death. The redhead Rosanna beating the flames off of her, yet worried about her friend.

And his partner, seriously injured.

Parker…he would survive, the doctor had said. But would he ever recover? Would he walk again? Be able to go back on the street?

He closed his eyes, wondering how he would feel if he had been in Parker's place. He lived and breathed his job. He'd be lost without it.

Yet lately he'd been filled with restless energy. With the need for something more.

Hell, he just missed having a family. A father who was alive. A mother who spoke to him. A brother who didn't hate him.

A woman who…wanted him. At least for a night.

Rosanna's face materialized in his mind, and his body hardened. She had felt so light and fragile in his arms, her voice raspy, but as whispery soft as an angel's. And those eyes, they had mesmerized him and turned him inside out. When she'd touched his hand to comfort him about Parker, a hot feeling had splintered through him.

Hunger.

Even with her face and hands stained with soot, and her red hair tangled and smoky, he had thought naughty things.

Like how the soft silkiness of her hair would feel against his belly. The way her delicate hand had felt pressed against his chest, holding on to him. Clutching him. Needing him. How it would feel if she'd moved it lower.

He hadn't wanted to leave her, not with the way she'd cried in his arms when he'd had to reveal the awful truth that her friend hadn't survived.

He'd seen guilt in her eyes, too.

Guilt he understood. Guilt he related to. Guilt forced him to get up in the morning and keep fighting criminals.

A life that had robbed him of morality, female companionship and a future that evolved around nothing but dealing with other bastards.

Still, like the bastard he was, when he closed his eyes again and inhaled the salty air, he saw Rosanna reaching for him, stripping naked and climbing into his bed.

Begging him to take her.

But she had nearly died tonight. Was a material witness in a possible arson case. A case he had to crack.

He could not get involved with her. Not

even for a quick, one-night interlude. Not even if visions of her naked taunted him for the rest of his life.

He gripped the edge of the chair as a disturbing thought struck him. Rosanna Redhill had been present at both fires tonight.

So had her friend Natalie.

He needed to question her again. One motive for arson was revenge. If she wasn't involved in the arson, she or her friend might be connected to the man who'd started it. And she definitely might have seen the man who'd set the fires...

GHOSTS ROSE from the grave stalking toward Rosanna, their hollowed, brittle bones rattling in the wind, their bulging eyes staring at her with accusations, their screams of terror echoing through the rows of tombstones.

Natalie was there. Shocked and searching, wondering what had happened, still not ready to accept that her young life had ended so unexpectedly.

Her voice whispered for help, pleading with Rosanna to save her, to bring her back to life.

To find her killer.

Rosanna jerked awake, perspiration soaking the hospital nightgown, her breath rushing from her chest in erratic puffs. She blinked against the darkness, and a tingle of alarm rippled through her. She felt someone's presence in the room, felt an undercurrent of a spirit's energy charging the air. Smelled the lingering fragrance of Natalie's jasmine perfume.

Crazy. She might have thought she'd made that firepoker move years ago, but she hadn't. And she certainly had never communed with the dead or had visits from ghosts. She'd never even felt a spirit's presence before.

Well, except for Granny Redhill…

Inhaling to calm herself, she detected another odor. Masculine. Sweat. Smoke.

Danger.

She jerked her head around, certain she'd find a man lurking in the room, but only shadows hovered in the corner.

The door stood slightly ajar though.

It had been closed when she'd finally succumbed to exhaustion and fallen asleep.

Perhaps the nurse had come in to check on

her. Or could someone else have been in her room?

Ridiculous. She did not have a stalker, ghost or otherwise. It was just her overactive imagination.

The room smelled like smoke because she hadn't showered since being pulled from the blaze. The masculine scent probably lingered from Detective Walsh's visit.

Shivering in spite of the heat, she rolled to her side facing the door, but she couldn't bring herself to close her eyes. She didn't want to have another nightmare, to see ghosts or Natalie's tormented expression, or hear her voice begging for help.

She wanted to turn the clock back and talk Natalie out of going to the Pink Martini.

And she wanted to see Detective Walsh again.

God, she *was* crazy.

But she would see him again, she thought with another frisson of panic. He'd ask questions. Want to know what she'd been doing at the club. Where she worked.

What if he looked into her past? What if he discovered the truth?

Her hands shook as she clutched the sheet to her chin. She'd have to be prepared. Answer curtly. Keep it to the point, focus on Natalie and what she'd seen at the bar.

Which had been nothing.

She'd tell him that, then he would leave and she would never have to see him again.

Then she would be safe.

And alone again just as she had always been.

Then she could explore this *gift,* if she really possessed one, and learn how to control it so she would never hurt anyone else again.

Determination gave her courage, and she finally relented to the fatigue draining her and fell asleep.

But when she awakened hours later, she was dreaming about the detective who had saved her from the burning building. This time he was making love to her, and she moaned in pleasure as he caressed her body with his hands, with his hungry kisses, and drove her into oblivion with the sweet lapping of his tongue across her nipples and inner thighs.

When she stirred awake, she saw him sitting in the chair beside her bed, quietly watching her. She could still feel the intense pounding of his body inside hers, the feel of his lips on her skin, the tremors of her orgasm from her dream. His eyes darkened as if he'd read her thoughts, knew the nature of her dreams.

The realization sent a flush to her face. In the next second, that flare of coldness settled back into his eyes, and she had the sudden urge to run from his scrutiny.

If he made her feel so rattled in her sleep, how would she react if he ever really touched her? And if he could turn cold in seconds flat, what would happen if he knew the truth about her?

BRADFORD STARED into Rosanna's sleepy gaze, his body hard from watching her sleep and hearing those tiny moans she'd elicited. When she'd first begun to sigh and claw at the covers, he'd thought she was having a nightmare about the fire. Reasonably so and expected.

Then that glass of water had tipped over, and spilled and he'd wondered what the hell had happened. She hadn't touched it and neither had he.

She must have bumped the table when she was twisting in the bed.

When he'd looked back at her, a slow smile had curved that delicate, pouty mouth, and she'd run her hands over her breasts and thighs. He'd realized then that her dreams were more gratuitous. Sexual maybe.

And those moans...they whispered of pleasure. Satisfaction. Arousal.

Which had excited the hell out of him.

Irritated at his body's traitorous response, he stifled a growl, shifting to hide the painful erection pressing against the fly of his jeans. Dammit. He was here to interrogate her, not drool over her body.

A very voluptuous, sexy body, he noted, thanks to that damn hospital gown coming untied and riding down her shoulder to reveal the delicious curve of one breast.

She cleared her throat, looking shaken. "Detective, how long have you been there?"

Long enough to know she was having sexy dreams. Who had been her lover?

Mentally shaking himself for wondering, he bit the inside of his cheek to keep from asking. He'd had no rest the night before. And seeing her, realizing how attracted to her he was, wasn't helping his mood.

He had no time for his libido. Not now.

Not with her.

"A few minutes," he said quietly, a little too gruffly for comfort. Then unable to help himself, he asked, "Were you having a nightmare?"

She jerked her gaze from his, but guilt and some other emotion he couldn't define colored her face. Had he not been so affected by her, he would have laughed.

He knew better than to play this game.

She seemed to notice that her gown had slipped then, and retied it, then yanked the sheet up to her chin. "I did earlier," she admitted in a somber voice.

The pain in her eyes sucker-punched him.

"I dreamed Natalie was calling me for help, but I was too late."

He clasped his hands together to keep from reaching for her. "There was nothing you could do."

Her soft sigh tore at him.

"If I'd only convinced her not to go to the club, she would be alive."

"So it was her idea to go?"

She nodded. "I'm not really into the club scene, but she begged me to accompany her. I thought she'd be safer if she didn't go alone. Has her family been notified?"

He nodded. "They're on their way. Can you talk about what happened?"

She swallowed as if gathering courage. "We both went in, ordered drinks. Natalie met a guy and they went to dance." She hesitated. "I watched from a corner table."

"Anybody with you?"

She shook her head. "I turned down a couple of drunk guys then went to the bathroom. Like I told you before, the fire started while I was inside the ladies' room."

He twisted his mouth in thought. "Did you know the guys who asked you to dance?"

She shrugged. "No. And they certainly weren't upset enough to get violent. I assume they moved onto the next girl."

Something in her tone sounded self-deprecating, but he decided not to explore it. "What about Natalie? Did she have a boyfriend who might have seen her with this other man and gotten jealous?"

She shook her head again. "No boyfriend. She just moved back here a few weeks ago."

"Where did she work?"

"She was interning at a design studio and taking classes at the Savannah College of Art & Design."

"What about you?"

She clamped her teeth over her lower lip for a minute. "I own a shop called Mystique. We sell specialty gifts, New Age books, stories of local folklore and ghost legends, candles, voodoo kits and dolls."

He frowned, still mesmerized by her eyes but disturbed by her answer. So she was into that New Age crap. Probably believed in the supernatural and local ghost legends.

"How did you and Natalie meet?"

She hesitated again, this time looked away as if she didn't want to answer.

"She visited the store," she finally said quietly.

He waited, wondering, testing to see if she'd fill the silence and volunteer more information. Instead tension vibrated between them. She didn't fit the profile of an arsonist, and didn't seem like the vindictive type to set a fire to hurt anyone. But it still struck him as odd that she'd been present at both scenes.

Although she'd given him no reason to think she or Natalie had been targets or that she knew the arsonist, he definitely wanted to find out more about Rosanna Redhill. What made her tick, what made her so intriguing, what made him want to hold her when they had nothing in common.

Why he wanted to ask if she had a boyfriend or any lovers when it probably had nothing to do with the case.

Why he sensed she was hiding secrets, that she wasn't at all the innocent angel she appeared to be.

Chapter Five

Rosanna hated to lie to the detective about how she'd met Natalie, but she'd detected disapproval when she'd mentioned her store.

She'd met the same instantaneous dislike before. People were either open to paranormal and supernatural phenomenon or they weren't. Because of his job, Detective Walsh analyzed facts and evidence, although she'd bet he used his gut instincts more often than he realized.

Still, she'd also agreed not to discuss the CIRP experiment outside the clinic. Besides, the project and the circumstances surrounding her friendship with Natalie had nothing to do with her friend's death.

He was watching her as if he expected her to say more when the doctor strode in.

The detective moved to the window while

the doctor checked her vitals. "How are you feeling?" he asked.

"All right," Rosanna said, although her ankle still felt stiff and achy. "I'm ready to go home."

He nodded. "I'll get the discharge paperwork ready."

Remembering that her dress had been ruined and that they'd cut it off of her when she arrived, she clung to the bedsheet. "Doctor, do you think one of the nurses might find me a robe or something to wear home?"

He gave a quick nod, and whisked out the door.

The detective turned back to face her. "I'll give you a lift home."

She knotted her hands by her side. "That's not necessary."

"Why? Do you already have a ride?"

She hesitated, considering another lie but sensed he would be able to read her. "No, but I can call a taxi."

"I said I'd drop you off," he said in a clipped tone.

She wanted to refuse, but didn't want to draw suspicion. Not that he had any reason to suspect her of anything.

No one knew about her past. It had been buried with her grandmother and would stay buried.

The doctor appeared with discharge papers in order. A nurse rushed in with a smile, and dropped a cotton robe on the foot of the bed. "An extra," she said. "One of the discount stores in town donates them."

"Thank you. I really appreciate it." She quickly slid her arms in the robe and belted it tight. Grateful the paramedics had found her purse, she grabbed it. The nurse gestured for her to take the wheelchair.

"I can walk," Rosanna argued.

"Hospital policy," the nurse said cheerfully.

Rosanna reluctantly relented, feeling vulnerable as the woman wheeled her to the elevator. The detective walked silently beside her, a force of such power that her insides fluttered with nerves.

The short ride to her apartment felt strained. Detective Walsh was so big and masculine that his body filled the small confined space. And his masculine scent made her stomach tighten, made her more aware of how naked she was below the robe and gown.

He parked in her driveway, then rushed around to help her out. She hated to accept his outstretched hand, but the moment she put weight on her foot, pain shot through her ankle and up her leg.

"You're hurt?" he asked in a dark voice.

"It's just a light sprain," she said, shrugging off his concern. "I'll be fine."

"Do you have any family or friends to stay with?" he asked as he assisted her onto the stoop.

She dug her keys from the bag and unlocked the door, smiling as her black cat, Shadow, darted up to welcome her. She leaned over and petted his back, then straightened to dismiss the detective. "No, but I'll be fine. Thanks for dropping me off."

He nodded and handed her a business card. "If you think of anything else, remember anyone who looked suspicious, please give me a call."

"I will." She leaned against the doorjamb. "Do you really think someone set that fire on purpose?"

His expression hardened. "We're investigating the possibility."

"But why would someone try to burn

down the bar, especially when it was filled to capacity?"

"Motives for arson vary. Insurance. Revenge. To cover another crime." His gruff voice grew lower. "Excitement is a possibility, too. Some arsonists feed on the energy of the fire."

She frowned, thinking about his statement, about some of the participants in the research study. One of the doctors had discussed energy, specifically psychic energy, mind over matter...

"We're still questioning everyone at the bar, and later today, we meet with the crime scene investigators." He twisted sideways for a minute, scanned the sidewalk as if checking to make sure the area was secure. "We'll talk to her family, but if you learn anything else about your friend from them, maybe the name of an old boyfriend or lover, let me know."

"I'll ask them." Her throat felt thick with grief as she remembered Natalie. Her family would be flying in, making funeral arrangements....

He lifted his hand as if he might touch her, then his gaze penetrated her, caressing her body all over as if his fingers had actually brushed her skin.

Her breath caught, and she started to lean toward him, but he dropped his hand back to his side, and jerked his eyes away as if he felt the pull of attraction between them and didn't like it, either. "Like I said, call me if you think of anything."

She nodded, then watched him walk back to his car. She had no idea why her body was reacting so strongly to him, why her nipples had stiffened as he looked at her and heat had pooled between her thighs, making her ache like she'd never ached before.

Why the thought of him leaving sent a frisson of fear and sadness through her.

She didn't need a relationship, or a complication in her life right now.

Especially a sexy one who made her want things she could never have. One who came with a badge and questions that she didn't want to answer.

BRADFORD SPENT the next three hours running background searches on the bar owner and the attendants, then questioned each of them in person, coordinating efforts with two other officers assigned to the case.

Later that afternoon, he grabbed a cup of coffee and met the captain, several other officers and the arson and crime scene investigators in one of the conference rooms.

Captain Black took the lead by relaying the latest news on Parker. "He's still in critical condition, but they've removed the ventilator and he's breathing on his own, so that's the good news." Black hesitated, a somber expression on his face. "The bad news is that he's not out of the woods yet so everyone send up prayers. Now, let's have a recap on what we have so far." He turned to Bradford, gesturing for him to speak.

Bradford took a sip of coffee to wash down the guilt over his partner's injuries. "The owner of the bar appears to be clean. No financial problems, heavy debts, prior problems with the law or gambling issues. Only possible flag is a divorce, but his wife isn't pinching him. I can't see him burning down his bar to collect insurance, not and risk lives and homicide charges."

"Anyone suspicious on your list?" Black asked.

"Struck out so far."

His coworkers offered similar reports.

"So no one saw anyone set the fire," Black said. "Then how did it get started?"

"The bar has a smoking section," a young rookie speculated.

"So you think someone dropped a cigarette and the place went up in flames?" Black asked.

One of the crime scene investigators, a female named Marcy Lucerne, spoke up. "The fire seemed to have spread too rapidly for that. There were also indicators of more than one point of origin, that the fire started in at least three different locations within the bar."

"So, our unknown subject, UNSUB, walked around the room dropping cigarettes or lit matches?" Bradford asked, not quite picturing that scenario.

Lucerne shrugged. "I'm just telling you what the evidence shows. Problem is, trace found no signs of an accelerant."

"The alcohol in the bar was the perfect accelerant," Bradford muttered.

A debate between the officers over theories broke out, but Black silenced them.

"All right, all right. This is not helping. We need more facts, some concrete evidence. Two people were killed in that fire and one of our own seriously injured." He paused. "Anything new on the other three fires?"

A negative response rippled through the room.

"Detective Walsh, it's my understanding that you've researched arsonists. Can you give us a preliminary profile of our suspect?"

Bradford winced internally, wondering how many of his fellow officers here knew his history. Black did, and had accepted him without question. But some of the others might not be so amenable.

"Certainly." He stood, faced the group, trying to recall the details he'd learned as his brother's criminal activities had become evident.

"Arson is the nation's fastest growing crime. Around fifty percent of arsonists are under eighteen years of age. If adults, most are in their twenties, never over thirty-five. Ninety percent are males, seventy-five percent white." He paused, trying to focus on the present, on helping Parker. Not on picturing Johnny's face in his mind.

"Most are from lower income, working class families. If they're middle class, motive is usually vandalism or excitement. Those are the most dangerous ones."

"What about their family history?" Lucerne asked.

"Absent or abusive father, emotional problems and problems with family and/or the mother. Guy may have struggled in school, have a learning disability, be a social misfit, appear physically or emotionally weak next to his peers."

"Type of job or profession?" Black asked.

"Most choose subservient work and then resent it."

"So we're not looking for a rocket scientist?" the rookie asked. "Maybe a druggie?"

Bradford shook his head. "Drugs are usually not a factor, although the firestarter probably has a criminal history of some kind. Motives vary. Setting a fire for revenge purposes usually occurs when someone feels they've been wronged, therefore, it's more personal. Fires to collect insurance occur when a person is in heavy debt. And sometimes firestarters want to cover up another crime."

"So far we don't think the bar fire fits in any of those categories, do we?" Black asked.

"Insurance seems unlikely," Bradford said. "And the owner claimed he didn't have any enemies, but we'll investigate that angle further."

Black gestured to Fox, and he nodded that he'd check it out.

"Vandalism is a possibility," Bradford continued, "although younger kids and teens usually target educational facilities such as schools or homes of other kids they know, classmates they don't like."

"What about arson for excitement?" Fox asked.

"A real possibility here. The firestarter usually targets public areas where he can watch, like parks, residential neighborhoods. The club last night fits that scenario." Bradford cleared his throat. "This type of firestarer is the most dangerous and hardest to trace. His target doesn't have to be connected to him in any way. This guy has a compulsion, may appear to be a psychopath with no conscience. He slips into an obsessive-compulsive dissociative trance when starting the fire and gets off on watching its destruction. It's a sexual thrill for him that may grow more intense." He was painting a bleak picture, but they had to know what they were up against.

"Meaning he needs the event to be bigger and more dramatic each time to get him off?" Black scowled.

Bradford nodded. "Exactly. And this UNSUB is good. So far he hasn't left signs of an accelerant or any trace evidence behind."

Black rapped his knuckles on the desk. "Let's get on this before this guy strikes again and hurts someone else."

The meeting dispersed, and Bradford headed back to his desk. He wished like hell they'd get a lead, that one of the spectators or Rosanna would remember something.

The image of her hobbling up the steps, wearing nothing but that flimsy hospital gown and robe rode through his head, and he went to his computer.

He'd run a background check on her and see what he found out, see if she had any skeletons in her closet, what she might be hiding.

He'd been a cop too long not to trust his instincts. She had been lying about something and he intended to find out the nature of that lie, and the reason for it.

Chapter Six

ROSANNA RESTED FOR a while, but nervous energy kept her from relaxing. That and nightmares of Natalie and the fire.

Shadow curled up next to her and Rosanna stroked the space between his ears, making him purr and close his eyes contentedly. Remembering the meeting at CIRP with the other research project members, she dragged herself from bed, showered and dressed in a sundress, then fed her cat and called a taxi.

A half hour later, curiosity rooted her to the seat as five members of the experiment gathered in a seated circle to discuss their expectations of the project.

Each of these five people believed they possessed some sort of special ability. The study consisted of other small groups focusing on various talents, as well as another group being given an experimental drug scientists believed would enhance chemicals in the brain and stimulate natural sensory abilities that people already possessed but normally didn't access.

She had never openly discussed what had happened with her father years ago, and had tried to suppress any gift she might possess for fear she might hurt someone else. Only Granny had known because of her sixth sense. Granny had also caught Rosanna experimenting in her bedroom, trying to move a book. But Rosanna had failed, and had been relieved that she had. She'd hoped her memory of her father's death was skewed by childhood trauma, that she hadn't actually caused the objects to move, and killed him.

But through the years, she'd experienced moments where, when she was upset, odd things had happened—a glass spilled over and shattered or a picture fell off the wall. In joining the study, she hoped to prove that these were coincidences, not a power she possessed.

A power that would make her a freak.

The thirty-something, sandy-haired Dr. Klondike folded her hands. "I'd like for each of you to describe your special ability."

Tension thrummed through the room as everyone shifted in the metal chairs. Apparently the others shared her anxiety over revealing themselves.

"I understand your hesitancy," Dr. Klondike said, offering a smile. "Most of you have probably faced ridicule and skepticism when you've discussed your special ability. But you're safe here. Your confidentiality is well guarded, and no one is going to pass judgment on you."

Rosanna relaxed slightly. True. They had signed confidentiality clauses prohibiting them from discussing the study or any individual's personal skills.

A beautiful, curvaceous girl in her early twenties with cornrows raised her hand. "I have dreams that come true," Shamera admitted. "Some are good, some aren't."

Dr. Klondike patted Shamera's hand in encouragement. "Those are premonitions," she explained. "You aren't making those things happen, Shamera. But in sleep, you're relaxed and your mind is open enough to tap into the psychic energy you possess."

The man next to her, a thin, wiry fellow with curly brown hair and a goatee spoke up next. "My name is Terrance. Sometimes I can read people's minds."

Everyone shifted, restless again.

He laughed. "That's why I don't like to tell people. My last girlfriend wanted me out of her head."

A ripple of laughter filtered through the room.

"But it's not like I read everyone or that I can control it. Sometimes it drives me crazy. I have so many voices in my head; I can't sort them out or even think. Sometimes I hear things I don't want to hear."

"We can help you learn to focus," Dr. Klondike said.

He jiggled his foot, his eyes twitching nervously.

The third member, a pale-faced emaciated woman clenched her hands in her lap. "I can float outside my body."

"You mean levitate?" Dr. Klondike asked.

"I don't know what you call it, but when I sleep, I leave my body and float above it. I actually watch myself and can see if someone comes in the room."

"I talk to the dead," a sixty-something lady with gold spangled earrings blurted.

"Ghosts, they come to me day and night wanting me to help them move on. Wanting me to talk to their loved ones for them."

"So we'll be working with you as a medium," Dr. Klondike said, turning to Rosanna.

Rosanna licked her dry lips. "I can move things, at least I did once a long time ago," she said quietly. "I think it's called telekinesis."

"That's right," Dr. Klondike said. "You said you did it a long time ago?"

The memory of her father coming toward her, the firepoker flying from the wall, then the deer head, flashed back. But she couldn't reveal the details. "When I was four. But my father said I had the devil in me, and I haven't done it since."

Compassion radiated from the doctor while others muttered similar comments they'd received.

"My mother claimed I was possessed," the medium said. "She tried to perform an exorcism to rid me of evil."

"My family thought I was schizophrenic," Terrence admitted. "They kept me drugged for years. I joined this study, hoping to get off of the meds because they make me so tired I can't function."

"My grandmother and aunt are both voodoo priestesses," Shamera said quietly. "I inherited my ability from them."

Rosanna thought of her own grandmother, the daughter of a Native American shaman who had a special gift of healing. Other stories about gifted Native Americans echoed in her head. A witch doctor who healed by touch. A warrior whose hearing was so astute he could hear an attack coming from miles away. A brave who could walk on fire without getting burned. Another who could throw flames with his fingertips.

Dr. Klondike turned to another man on her left. He was tall, thin with neatly clipped brown hair, dressed in nice slacks with a button-down blue shirt. He'd been listening quietly, looking distant. "And you, sir?"

He cut his gaze toward Rosanna for a brief second, and a shiver rippled through her. His eyes, behind the horn-rimmed glasses, were a cobalt-ice-blue.

"Kevin," he said in a slightly nasally voice as he whipped his head back toward the doctor. "I can freeze things with my hands."

The mind reader cleared his throat and shifted restlessly, and out of the corner of her eye, Rosanna saw his eyes widen briefly.

Kevin gave him a cold look. "What are you doing?"

The mind reader gripped the edges of the chair. "Uh…nothing. I just had something in my throat."

Tension stretched between the two men, and Rosanna wondered if the mind reader had tapped into Kevin's thoughts. She fidgeted, reminded herself that she should guard her own thoughts from the man.

"We're off to a great start here," Dr. Klondike said calmly as if to dispel the anxiety. "We'll meet twice a week for support sessions, and each of you will set up individual appointments. Don't forget before you leave to stop by the lab. We need another blood sample for testing."

The initial tension had dissipated, and everyone stood, making eye contact, and offering smiles of acceptance.

Dr. Klondike approached Rosanna. "Miss Redhill, we're holding a special session on telekinesis now if you can stay."

Rosanna nodded and followed her into an

adjoining room where ten other people had taken seats. For the next hour the doctor in charge, a rail-thin salt-and-pepper haired man named Dr. Salvadore, led a discussion on mind over matter, which rolled into a hands-on experiment where he challenged each participant to concentrate on his or her skill.

Rosanna focused intently but was unable to even move a pencil. "Maybe I was wrong and I'm not telekinetic." She hoped that was true. Then she could let go of her guilt.

"If you haven't actively used your powers, they may be weak," the doctor explained. "Sometimes people who don't understand their abilities think their gift is evil, but it's not. It's scientifically based. Humans only use ten percent of their brains. That's the reason for our study. We believe the brain is being wasted, and those with special abilities can be useful to the world. Using that gift just requires taking control of mind over matter." Dr. Salvadore gave her a quick pat of encouragement. "It takes time and practice to learn to draw on your energy and hone your skill."

"The only time I've ever felt I could move

objects was when I was really angry or upset," Rosanna admitted.

The doctor smiled knowingly. "Because you unconsciously accessed a part of your brain that you normally don't use. That anger released endorphins, which caused you to drop your barriers, lose control of your inhibitions and utilize your power."

His theory made sense.

Some of the others failed at their first attempts as well. A young boy in his teens seemed to be the strongest. He summoned a penny, then a pencil, then finally moved a notebook across the table, drawing applause from the participants.

As the session ended, Rosanna left the room, not surprised to see two other rooms emptying with other groups dispersing. She headed to the lab, dread clenching her stomach at the thought of having blood drawn again. When she'd made her initial visit to the research park, a gangly guy named Louis had drawn her blood. While he put a Band-Aid on her arm, he'd invited her to dinner. She'd turned him down, then felt guilty later because he'd looked deflated. But she'd been too nervous about the experiment to accept a social invitation with someone who worked at the center.

This time, a slender woman in her early twenties with gray-green eyes drew her blood, and Rosanna relaxed, grateful not to have to face an awkward meeting with Louis.

Relieved, she limped to the front desk and asked the receptionist to call a taxi to drive her to her shop. Outside, the hot summer air caused her hair to stick to the back of her neck. She lifted it with one hand and fanned herself, then removed a water bottle from her bag. She drank deeply as others from the experiment filed outside and walked past her heading to their cars.

Beside her, a small fire erupted in the trash can. She jumped up, and doused the flames with her water.

She hadn't noticed anyone smoking or near the receptacle…

That strange feeling of being watched crept up her spine again. Her heart racing, she glanced around and saw a man disappearing around the corner.

The conversations from her meeting rolled through her head. The special gifts and powers. The Native American folk legends she had heard from her grandmother. One in particular nagged at her memory banks. The flamethrower. The small warrior had so much heat in his body that he didn't need flint to create tiny sparks of fire. Flaming Hands, they called him, because he simply had to focus, concentrate and draw upon the heat and energy in his body and the fire would combust. In the legend, he used his power not only to keep the tribe warm, but when they were attacked by soldiers, he'd staved off the attack by throwing fireballs at the enemy.

She stared at the burning trash. Was it possible that someone in one of the groups here possessed that ability?

No…that was crazy. Someone must have dropped a cigarette inside the wastebasket, and it had simply taken a few minutes for it to catch fire…

BRADFORD WAS STILL contemplating the information he'd found on Rosanna Redhill when he stopped by her shop. Her father had died suspiciously at their house when she was four years old.

Apparently he had suffered a head injury from a firepoker and a bookcase had fallen on him and crushed his internal organs.

Bradford had discovered an article about the death with a photo of Rosanna included. She had been such a fragile looking child with that wild red curly hair and those luminous big green eyes. Instantaneous compassion for her had filled him.

Her story disturbed him and triggered more questions. She had been alone in the house when her father died. According to police reports, she had been traumatized, and unable to tell them who had killed her father.

A neighbor had heard the commotion, come over and discovered Mr. Redhill's dead body on the floor. According to her, Rosanna's mother hadn't been around for years.

Although police had finally located her, she had given up all rights to Rosanna, so the four-year-old had been sent to live with her grandmother in Savannah, and had undergone counseling. But she'd never divulged the details of her father's murder.

Even more interesting, her grandmother had been a practicing witch doctor.

Bradford was well aware that Savannah had a diverse cultural makeup, including the Gullah people, believers in the supernatural, and followers of witchcraft and voodoo.

Rosanna Redhill's shop, Mystique, obviously catered to that population. A bell tinkled on the door as he entered the store, a mixture of scents assaulting him. He quickly scanned the room for Rosanna, but didn't see her so he assumed she'd stayed home to rest. A teenager with a half dozen piercings, tattoos and burgundy hair worked the register, while a few customers roamed the store.

Candles, herbs, roots and God only knew what else filled shelves, which lined the room. Sage, Sandalwood, St. John's Wart, salt, saffron, mandrake root, leek, hemlock, graveyard dust, toad's legs, raven's blood, rabbit's ears, witches grass wormwood... The list went on and on.

The selection of candles and oils was just as varied with names like Master Candle, Court Candle, Black Devil Candle, Black Serpent Candle, Lucky Oils, Money Oil, Black Powers Oil, Passion Oil...

All ingredients for voodoo and witchcraft spells.

Books about Reiki, voodoo and witchcraft, and recipes for magic spells filled one wall while a wide array of voodoo dolls, gris-gris, masks and mojos occupied another corner. To the left, he noted a section housing books about local ghost legends, Native American folklore and hand-woven baskets created by the Gullah people along with gift items including a collection of herbal and medicinal teas, aromatherapy candles and bath products.

The bell tinkled again, and he pivoted and saw Rosanna limp inside, carrying an oversize mustard-yellow bag over her shoulder. Today she wore a dark green sundress and sandals, with her hair pulled back at her nape with a ribbon. His gut tightened, his awareness of her natural beauty striking him again.

Yet she looked troubled about something, deep in thought, even shaken.

She's grieving for her friend, he reminded himself. And judging from the dark circles beneath her eyes, she hadn't rested when he'd left her at her apartment.

She glanced up and saw him, and a wary expression clouded her eyes.

That nagging feeling that she was hiding something returned to dig at him.

With her troubled background and up-bringing, she might have serious issues, maybe even psychological problems stemming back to the day her father died. He'd read about children who'd witnessed a parent's murder at a young age and re-pressed the memory, and the devastating effects the trauma could have on the psyche.

Yet one more reason for him to treat her with suspicion and to avoid a personal in-volvement with her.

ROSANNA WILLED herself not to react to the detective, but the sight of his dark, intense eyes boring down on her made her squirm. She felt as if he could read her mind, and he knew that he made her nervous.

Between the club last night and the small fire in the trash bin at CIRP that had erupted out of nowhere, she was plenty antsy. "De-tective Walsh?" Rosanna asked as she ap-proached him. "Did you find out who set the fire at the bar?"

His jaw tightened. "Not yet, we're still investigating."

She clutched her bag tightly, maneuvering the merchandise aisles until she reached the register. Something about his breath, his scent, the whisper of his husky voice drew her. But judging from the scowl on his face as he skeptically examined a book of love potions, he disapproved of her store and its contents.

Inhaling a deep breath, she smiled at Honey, one of her salesgirls, and gestured that she'd take command of the register. Honey grinned and went to straighten merchandise and greet customers.

Feeling calmer with the space between them, she turned back to the detective. "How can I help you?"

"Have you'd talked to Natalie's parents?"

Emotions flooded her throat. "Yes, on my cell phone on the way over here. They're devastated."

He gave a clipped nod. "Understandable."

"She was their only child." Rosanna clamped her teeth over her lower lip to keep from spilling out the terrible grief churning through her.

"Did they mention funeral arrangements?"

"They're holding a small memorial

service at the Savannah Methodist Church at 2:00 p.m. tomorrow afternoon."

"Thanks. I assume you're going?"

She fiddled with one of the voodoo dolls on the counter. "Yes, they asked me to sing." Now why had she told him that?

"You sing at church?"

A flush scalded her neck. "You sound surprised?"

"I just don't see you as the religious type."

"Why not?"

He gestured around her shop with a scowl.

Her hackles rose. "Most beliefs in witch-craft, voodoo and New Age theories are based on spirituality, Detective."

He didn't look convinced. "I didn't mean to insult you. It was just an observation."

A tense second passed.

"I'm sure it means a lot to them to know that she had friends," he finally said.

Another wave of guilt washed over her. She wished she could have done something to prevent Natalie's death. If she had a gift why couldn't she have been psychic, had a premonition that a fire was going to destroy the place…

He was studying her again when she

looked up. "Did you happen to remember anything else? Anyone suspicious at the bar or at Cozy's Café earlier?"

She contemplated confessing that she thought someone had been following her lately, and about the waste bin fire at CIRP but bit her tongue. She had no concrete reason to believe that the incident was related to last night, or to her. He would think she was crazy if she started talking about legendary firestarters. "No."

He shifted, jammed his hands into his pockets. "Then I guess I'll see you tomorrow at the funeral."

Surprised, she had to swallow before she spoke. "You're coming to Natalie's memorial service?"

He nodded, his expression grave. "Sometimes criminals attend the funeral of their victim."

The realization that the person responsible for Natalie's death might actually show up to watch her friend be buried sent a shiver through Rosanna. "That's creepy."

He nodded. "But true. I want to watch the crowd, talk to her parents, see if anyone looks out of place or suspicious. If the killer is there, maybe we'll get lucky and catch the bastard."

HE STOOD OUTSIDE Mystique, rolling the cigarette between his thumb and forefinger, his senses tuned as he watched Detective Bradford Walsh leave the store. The tobacco popped and ignited between the heat of his fingers. He watched the tip light up, then brought the cigarette to his lips. The smell of smoke engulfed him, heating his body with an unquenchable lust.

He itched to set another fire, to watch it take more property with it, to watch the fear in victim's faces, to hear their screams of terror and pain.

And death.

Oh, the sweetness of it…

Only Walsh—Brad boy—was determined to stop him. He wouldn't succeed, though. The detective didn't have a clue who he was up against.

A drop of perspiration beaded on his face, and he swiped at it, angry that one little redhead and a geek who called himself a mind reader could make him sweat. He would not be discovered.

He would show all those bullies from school, all those pigs who'd arrested him when he was younger, and Brad boy that he was smart, a force to be reckoned with. Now he'd fine-tuned his special ability, he could not be stopped,

Ever.

He was too talented, too smart, too good at disguising himself and not leaving evidence.

Those doctors at CIRP had helped him immensely. More than they knew.

She had been there, too. Rosanna Redhill. Room 313. A part of the project.

So, what was her story?

Tension thrummed through his muscles. He flexed his fingers, then extended them, focusing on the napkin in the trash until it sparked and erupted. Laughter bubbled in his throat as it turned to ashes.

He'd find out more about Rosanna, what she was up to.

And that mind reader, Terrance. The man had nailed his coffin shut when he'd invaded *his* mind.

Chapter Seven

Rosanna tossed and turned all night, more nightmares of the fire that had killed her friend alternating with images of Detective Walsh exposing her as the devil child who had caused her father's death.

After her trip to CIRP, she'd spent hours researching paranormal abilities and activities on the Internet. She'd located a Web site where individuals had posted interesting stories of unusual events and noted entries of shapeshifters being spotted, of hauntings, raising the dead, magic spells, body possessions, psychics, telekinesis, orbing and firestarters.

She understood Bradford Walsh's skepticism. As she'd read some of the more outlandish entries, she wondered how many were legitimate and how many might be bogus.

She spent the morning at the shop, but left Honey to watch the store while she attended Natalie's memorial service.

Mr. and Mrs. Gorman sat somber and teary-eyed as she stood to the right of Natalie's casket and began the first verse of "Amazing Grace."

Nerves knotted her stomach as she stared at the small gathering. Natalie hadn't lived in Savannah long enough to have formed a large network of friends, but two college girlfriends had driven down from Atlanta, and a former boyfriend sat beside them.

Detective Walsh slid into a pew near the back, and her voice faltered slightly. She had to block out his presence before she could continue for fear he would hear her voice shaking and realize how strongly he affected her.

Finally ending the song, she headed to the pew behind Natalie's parents, but the detective's comment about the arsonist attending the service made her skim the crowd. Was the person who'd killed her friend here now?

Had he known Natalie, or had she been a random victim of his sick, twisted mind?

BRADFORD STUDIED the mourners gathered at the church with an eagle's eye, hoping someone would stand out, but he'd been in law enforcement long enough to realize the killer would not announce his presence.

Unless he decided to leave a calling card of some kind. So far, he hadn't. No evidence or clues. No accelerant.

But if he were truly a serial arsonist, he would strike again. Eventually he might become cocky enough to screw up.

Then Bradford would catch him.

His gut had tightened as he'd listened to Rosanna's sultry voice, and his body had flamed with heat as her eyes met his. Her voice had sounded angelic, and now she appeared to be listening intently to the preacher's eulogy. Natalie's parents huddled together, their grief a palpable force in the room.

He half listened to the reverend's words, distracted by Rosanna wiping tears from her cheeks. He had the insane urge to join her, to place his hand over hers and comfort her.

The service ended with a prayer, and the pallbearers carried the coffin down the aisle. Bradford waited until the room emptied, then followed the caravan of vehicles to the cemetery outside of Savannah.

The afternoon sun beat down on the brittle grass, blades crunching between his boots as he crossed the grounds. More words from the pastor, sniffles and condolences as Natalie's friends spoke to her parents. He glanced around the graveyard, memorizing faces, searching the perimeter and woods beyond. He thought he noticed a shadow move between the oaks but couldn't be sure, so he moved slightly to the left, ready to give chase if needed.

Rosanna placed a rose on Natalie's grave, hugged Natalie's parents, then waded through the rows of graves to the edge of the crowd.

Unable to help himself, he inched near her.

"Did you see anyone suspicious?" she asked softly.

He shook his head, once again darting a glance toward the thick, tall oaks and pines.

Suddenly a shriek rent the air, followed by another. People scurried away from the grave. As the group parted, Bradford's eyes widened.

A thin streak of fire sprang up out of

nowhere, then rippled in a circle around Natalie's grave, flames dancing wildly as they caught the dry grass.

ROSANNA HAD NEVER seen anything so bizarre. A wind suddenly rattled the trees and sent twigs and leaves fluttering. She quickly scanned the panicked faces, shock and hysteria evident as everyone scattered.

"It's the spirits," someone shouted.

"The devil," an elderly woman whispered.

"Black magic," another woman muttered. "There must be a witch here."

"Or a voodoo priestess," someone else interjected.

"They're right," Rosanna said to Bradford. "The way the fire is encircling the grave looks like some kind of ritualistic ceremony…"

"That's ridiculous," Bradford snapped. "There is nothing paranormal going on here. We'll find a match or evidence of a lighter somewhere."

Rosanna pointed to the burning blades of grass. Even more disconcerting, she saw Dr. Klondike, Dr. Salvadore and Louis standing at the edge of the gathering, watching with avid interest. "But how did the person who set this make the fire spread in that circle?"

"I don't know yet. Maybe the arsonist came here before the service and spread lighter fluid on the ground or some kind of accelerant."

She frowned, contemplating his theory, while he held up his hands. "Police. No one leave the area."

Unfortunately some people had already reached their cars and were fleeing. Rosanna doubted the firestarter was still around; he'd probably taken off immediately. Two funeral attendants began shoveling dirt on the flames to extinguish them. Bradford quickly questioned the guests and examined the contents of their pockets and purses.

Several protests and complaints rippled through the group, and Natalie's parents shot him a look of disapproval, as if his tactic was somehow desecrating the sanctity of their daughter's memorial service. But whoever had started the fire had done that, and he told them so.

When he explained that he was looking for an arsonist who had caused the fire, the same one who might have killed their daughter, their attitudes changed.

Heat scalded Rosanna's face as she watched him interrogate the attendees. He found several people with matches and lighters and confiscated them for further testing, then jotted down contact information. The CSI team arrived, and he conferred with them before they began to take samples of the grass, ground and surrounding area.

She huddled beside Natalie's parents, uncertain how to comfort them.

"Detective Walsh really believes that someone set fire to that club intentionally, doesn't he?" Mrs. Gorman asked.

Rosanna nodded. "They're investigating that theory."

Tears glittered in the woman's grief-stricken eyes, making Rosanna's heart clench with sympathy. "Detective Walsh is a good cop, Mrs. Gorman. He'll find the answers."

Although he certainly didn't seem open to the possibility of a supernatural explanation.

Could she really blame him?

He was a man of the law, a man who dealt in cold, hard facts, a man who had to have proof to present to a court. Not legends of firestarters or spirits or people with superhuman abilities or powers.

Natalie's father swiped a handkerchief across his face, distraught. Emotion thickened Rosanna's throat. Natalie deserved some answers, and so did her parents.

Regardless of what the detective thought of her, she had to make him listen to her. Maybe it was time to tell him about the incident at CIRP and their experiments with the paranormal. But then she'd have to explain the reason she had joined the study.

And she wasn't sure she was ready to bring him into her confidence.

BRADFORD SCOWLED as the crime scene techs finished gathering samples. He'd ordered them to dig around the graves and check the woods, but so far they'd found nothing.

There had to be some logical explanation here, some chemical the arsonist had sprinkled on the lawn that would explain the circular fire.

The hoopla about the devil and black magic was crazy.

Natalie's parents had finally left, thanks to Rosanna's encouragement, and he had dismissed the other attendees, knowing in his gut that the firestarter had slipped away before he'd started interrogating the guests.

Rosanna still stood in the shadow of the funeral tent, her arms hugging herself as she stared at the mound of freshly turned earth covering her friend's coffin. A quiet tension settled over the graveyard as the sun waned, and a gray cloud the color of the granite markers floated across the sky.

He needed to leave, but felt compelled to comfort her. She seemed so lonely, like an exotic animal that didn't quite fit into the pack. That loneliness drew him, reminded him of the solitary nights he'd spent belaboring the reason his brother had turned to criminal activities, and his mother hated him.

She reminded him of the reason he continued to do what he did—hunt down criminals, psychos and perps.

She looked so damned innocent.

Feeling the pain radiating from her as if it were a knife pricking his own skin, he approached her, but with caution. "Rosanna?"

She inhaled deeply, making him well aware of her chest rising and falling, and the emotions warring within her.

He pressed a hand to her back to guide her away from the scene, but she turned to face him, eyes dark with pain and sadness. "Why did she die instead of me?"

Understanding caused his chest to clench. He'd been in the accident when his father had died. He'd wondered the same thing.

He should offer some comforting words about it not being her time, but old platitudes, especially religious ones, failed him and seemed callous anyway. "I can't answer that. But what you're feeling is normal. The psychologists refer to it as survivor's guilt. It's not uncommon, especially for victims of major crises like plane crashes, hurricanes…" He forced himself to shut up, knowing he sounded like a walking catalog of police knowledge. But subtlety had never been his strong suit.

As his mother had pointed out when he'd slapped the cuffs on his brother.

"I'm sorry," he said. "I didn't mean to sound like a psychology lecture."

A faint smile tugged at the corners of her

mouth. It was the first time he'd seen her come close to a smile, and it altered her appearance drastically, made her eyes light up and her even more beautiful. He wondered what she'd look like if she were truly happy. Excited.

Aroused.

Dammit. Why the hell was he thinking things like that about a victim, especially in the middle of a freaking graveyard? Maybe he'd lost all perspective…

"Thank you for trying," she said. "I must admit, I had no idea how to comfort Natalie's parents. What can you say when someone so young passes? Hopefully their faith will help them through the grieving process."

"You got your faith from your grand-mother?"

"Yes." Her eyes crinkled at the corners with a frown. "Why do you mention my grandmother?"

He shrugged, a million reasons flitting through his mind. She might look like an angel and sing like one, but that body and those eyes were bewitching. Seductive.

Made him want to forget the graveyard, the case, his logic, *everything* and take her to bed.

Which would not happen.

"Your shop, the fact that your grand-mother practiced as a witch doctor." He paused. "She had Native American blood in her, and so do you. And you moved in with her after your father died, didn't you?"

Fear glittered in her eyes, and she re-treated a step away from him as if she wanted to run. Too late, he realized he'd pushed too soon.

"You checked up on me?" she asked in a strangled voice.

His heart hammered with the realization that he'd hurt her. But he was a cop, and he had to explore every angle, treat everyone as a suspect.

He'd do the same if he had to do it over again.

"It's my job. I have to investigate every-one. Clear suspects. Study situations. Learn the truth."

Distrust and a deep fear darkened her eyes. "So I'm a suspect?"

"Everyone is a suspect until they're proven otherwise."

She sucked in a sharp breath. "You really think I had something to do with my friend's death? That I'm capable of trying to kill those innocent people?"

"It's not personal, Rosanna," he said. "I'm trying to find Natalie's killer."

"I want that, too," she whispered. "More than you'll ever know."

He wanted to believe her, but he sensed she was keeping something from him. Maybe a detail that might lead to the killer.

DISAPPOINTMENT stabbed at Rosanna, and she braced herself for another onslaught of skepticism. But she had to speak up, try to convince the detective to at least consider her ideas.

"Tell me what you're thinking," he said.

She sighed. "You don't trust anyone, do you?"

His eyes darkened. "No, I don't. What about you? After seeing your father murdered as a young child, you must have trust issues yourself."

Oh God, he *was* investigating her.

"I don't want to talk about my father." Suddenly feeling as if she was suffocating, she ran toward her car. She had to leave, get away. Go home alone and forget this insane attraction to him. He was a cop, and if he dug deep enough, he might learn the truth about her.

A truth she wanted to remain buried forever.

BRADFORD WATCHED Rosanna retreat with a dull ache mounting in his chest. She was scared, running from something. But what?

Pain had flickered in her eyes when he'd mentioned her father's murder, and he felt like a bastard for putting it there. She'd been just a kid when she'd lost her dad.

Maybe he had been cruel to mention the murder. But he wanted to know more about her. And the only way he could do that was to push because she certainly wasn't offering information freely.

He headed toward his car, climbed in and was driving back to the precinct when his cell phone rang. His captain. "Walsh."

"It's Black. There's another fire. This time it's a car."

"It wasn't an accident?" Bradford asked.

"I don't think so. Come and see for yourself." Black recited the address.

"I'll be right there." Bradford spun around

and raced into town, wondering if this fire was related to the others.

If so, he hoped to hell they caught a break this time and found the bastard.

Chapter Eight

Bradford watched the firemen extinguishing the blaze with a mixture of frustration and anger.

They'd been too late. The man in the car had died.

"His name is Terrance Shaver," one of the rescue workers said as he handed Bradford the man's ID. "The woman who called it in said that the car just burst into flames. Apparently the guy tried to get out, but the car exploded before he could make it."

Bradford surveyed the street, noting a handful of spectators watching in intrigued horror. His captain already had uniforms questioning them.

"Maybe faulty engine or something," Black suggested. "We'll have a team analyze the car."

"I want to talk to the woman who called it in." Bradford strode toward the middle-aged brunette sitting by the ambulance, looking shaken. A chocolate Lab lay panting at her feet.

He knelt at her eye level. "Ma'am, I'm Detective Walsh. Can you tell me what happened?"

She fidgeted with the collar of her shirt. "I was walking Sylvester and saw this guy rush out from his house. He was in such a hurry, he almost knocked me down. And he was nervous, kept looking around as if he was running from something."

Bradford frowned. "Did you see anyone else, maybe someone he was running from?"

"No," she said with a nervous laugh. "I was too busy trying to keep Sylvester under control. He started barking and tried to take off toward the house. It was the oddest thing. Sylvester's a softy. He *never* barks."

"Then what happened?"

"Why, the man climbed in his car, and locked the doors, his eyes wide like he was scared to death. Then he cranked the engine and the car burst into flames."

Her voice broke. "It was awful," she whispered. "Just awful. He screamed and tried to unlock the doors but the car erupted before he could escape."

Bradford swallowed. Obviously the fire had reached the gas tank and the man hadn't had a chance. But what had caused the car to burst into flames in the first place?

And what had spooked the man before he died?

ROSANNA STARED at the morning paper in horror. Another fire—this one a car on E. Taylor Street.

She'd met the man who'd died— Terrance Shaver.

She blinked, studying the photo with a sense of trepidation. She'd seen him before, from the CIRP experiment. He was the mind reader.

Her hands shook and she set her coffee cup down with a thud, then dropped into the kitchen chair to read the article. Natalie had died in a fire and was part of the experiment. She had nearly died in the same fire. And now another man who belonged to the group had lost his life.

It couldn't be a coincidence.

Detective Walsh and another officer, Captain Black, had both been present at the scene interviewing possible witnesses. A middle-aged woman reported that Terrance had run outside to his Toyota Camry looking spooked, climbed inside, locked the doors and started the engine. Then the car had mysteriously caught fire.

The man had tried to claw his way out, but the gas tank exploded and he hadn't had a chance.

A lump welled in her throat. She didn't really know Terrance Shaver, but the fact that she'd just met him made her feel connected to him somehow.

Connected to this whole mess.

She had to tell the detective that she knew him.

But what would he say? Would he jump to the conclusion that she had hurt the man?

She checked the time of death mentioned in the article and realized the detective must have driven straight from the funeral to the fire. She had gone back to her shop, so at least she had an alibi.

But how would she say she'd met

Terrance? Should she tell Detective Walsh about CIRP?

She'd signed that confidentiality clause…

Besides, so far the people she'd met in the project had seemed normal. A nervous laugh bubbled in her throat. Well, normal *except* for claiming to have powers. But none of them had seemed dangerous.

She pushed away her coffee, unable to stomach it now, not when her nerves were still in knots. She bunched her hair into a ponytail, grabbed her purse and hurried to her car. A few minutes later, one of the officers showed her into the detective's office.

His eyes widened when he saw her. "Rosanna? What are you doing here?"

The newspaper rattled in her hands as she laid it on the desk. "I saw the story about that car fire last night."

He glanced at it, then back at her. "Yes?"

She wet her lips, her throat suddenly dry. "I met that man Terrance."

His eyebrows shifted. "Really? When? Where?"

This was the tricky part. Telling him about the experiment meant revealing too much.

But didn't she owe it to Natalie to help if she could?

"Rosanna?"

"He was interested in paranormal occurrences, too," she said.

"That again?"

"Just hear me out. I know you may not believe in the supernatural," she began, "but I've seen things, people who have ESP, psychic abilities, the ability to do things other humans can't."

"Like your grandmother and her black magic?"

"Yes. She was a true healer." She paused, the disbelief in his eyes tearing a path of destruction through her bravado. Tormented by her own destiny, she felt cursed by her past and the heritage she'd only begun to explore, much less claim.

He folded his arms, a sheen of perspiration glistening on his stern brow. "And you've seen evidence of paranormal occurrences?"

"Yes."

He gave her a look that made her want to wilt. "So, tell me about them."

She licked her dry lips. "I met a woman

who communes with the dead. And this guy Terrance claimed he could read minds."

A muscle ticked in his jaw. "There are a lot of people who claim to do things they can't do, Rosanna. Believe me, I know. I once worked a case where a so-called psychic insisted she could help us find a missing person. The victim died because we were chasing that fraudulent lead…."

"I'm sorry," she said. "I can understand your skepticism. But this case is different. I read that eyewitness's statement." She took a deep breath, then continued, "She said the fire just sprang up out of nowhere. And yesterday I was…sitting on a park bench, and a fire suddenly started in the trash bin next to me."

His mouth thinned. "There are logical explanations for these things, Rosanna. We're checking the car to see if the engine was faulty. And someone probably dropped a cigarette butt into that trash."

"Maybe. But when I looked up I thought I saw someone disappearing around the corner."

He sighed. "Did you get a good look at him?"

"No. Then when I got home, I went online and researched paranormal behavior."

He gave her a deadpan look but she forged ahead.

"What I found was really interesting. I read about some guy whose body had such a strong electrical current that it threw off electricity in the house. He could touch things and make electricity spark to life."

"Rosanna." Disgust laced his voice. "I really don't have time for this."

She had to make him believe her. "In another case, a young boy had an unusually high body temperature—so high that heat radiated off of him. Sometimes he burned people with his touch. He was struck by lightning when he was younger."

She sighed, then continued, "When I was little, my grandmother also told me a legend about a firestarter, a Native American boy who had flaming hands. The energy from his body consumed him. He could pull upon the heat's power to start a fire. He could also throw fire with his hands, which helped save his tribe from a vicious attack. And researchers—"

He paced across the room, hissed, then

faced her again. "Rosanna," he said, cutting her off, "I think you need to see a therapist."

Hurt splintered through her. "I don't need a therapist. Just consider the possibility. Research is being conducted at different hospitals on the subject of paranormal phenomenon. There are Web sites everywhere with stories of incidents that can't be explained—"

"Those are fiction, evidence of people's overactive imaginations."

"No more so than people's belief in religion, in God or angels."

"But I deal in facts." He looked as if his patience had worn out.

She had to tell him about the project at CIRP.

But as soon as she opened her mouth, he stopped her with an upheld hand. "How about this theory—you're making up stuff to distract me. You've been present at three fires, and you're telling me about another one you saw yesterday that you failed to mention before. Maybe you know who this firestarter is and are trying to protect him."

She narrowed her eyes. "I would never do that. Not and let Natalie's killer go free."

He pulled a hand down his face. "Look," he said softly, more compassionately, "I understand that your father was killed when you were four, and you were traumatized. Maybe that past has made you unstable, but you should talk to someone. Get some help, Rosanna."

She'd been insane to think he might believe her.

If he saw your telekinetic power, he might.

But she couldn't expose that much of herself. Couldn't trust him with the truth, not with the way he was looking at her now. He'd obviously checked into her past, knew she'd been in counseling.

Did he know the reason? That the teachers had sent her to counseling because of drawings she'd done depicting scenes with witches and supernatural occurrences? That news would only feed his conviction that she needed mental help.

Besides, she had no idea if she was right, if a firestarter really existed or if one was here in Savannah and had killed her friend.

Still, it pained her that he didn't believe her. That he thought she might be covering for a killer…

BRADFORD MUTTERED an obscenity as Rosanna rushed from his office. Dammit, he hated to hurt her, but he really didn't have time for such nonsense.

He needed distance from her and lots of it to wrestle his libido back in control. Because in spite of her ridiculous theories, he was attracted to her.

And he liked that spitfire determination in her, the way her eyes smoldered when she tried to persuade him of her beliefs, the way her breath caught and her voice grew raspy with conviction.

Why the hell did the only woman he'd been attracted to in the past year have to be a nutcase?

Disgusted with the day's events and still contemplating how the car fire started, and even more curious, how the fire surrounding the grave had originated and created that odd circular pattern, he strode to his car, climbed in and drove to the hospital. Dark clouds hovered low in the sky, obliterating any sun and painting a gloomy picture that mirrored his mood.

At the information desk, he requested Parker's room number, and was informed that Parker was heavily sedated, but he was allowed visitation, limited to five minutes.

The bandages on his partner's face, hands and arms along with the machines pumping fluids and oxygen into him caused Bradford to hesitate at the door. Parker was a damn big guy, almost as big as Bradford. Seeing him lying in bed incapacitated sent a spasm of nausea through him.

Sucking in a deep breath, he forced his leaden feet forward. Parker deserved to be kept updated, in the loop on the investigation. He had a lot at stake in this case, and in spite of Bradford's mother's belief that he had no loyalty, that he would only disappoint those who counted on him, Bradford refused to let his partner down.

"Hey, buddy," he said in a low voice as he approached the bed.

Parker's eyelids twitched, but he didn't open them. Instead his deep breathing reverberated through the room, the drip of the IV steady and slow, as if that drip ticked off the seconds of Parker's life like sand through an hourglass.

"Okay, here's what we have so far," Bradford said, bracing his feet apart. He told him about the car fire and death the night before. "I'm not sure it's related to the other cases, but we'll see. So far we haven't connected the fires and can't prove arson, although with the bar, there's no doubt in my mind that the fire was set intentionally. According to the witnesses and CSI team, there was more than one point of origin."

He frowned, paced to the window and stared out at the ominous cloud cover. "Problem is there's no sign of an accelerant. My guess is that the alcohol served as one in the bar." He relayed what had happened at the cemetery. "That was the strangest thing I've ever seen, man. The way the flames burned in that circle around the grave…"

He hesitated, tried to regroup his thoughts. "And I have a feeling this arsonist was there, that he set that fire right in front of my eyes and I didn't see him set it." He ran a hand over his beard stubble. "But I don't see how that was possible."

Frustration underscored the breath he expelled. He wondered if Parker could hear him.

"But you're going to get a kick out of this.

Rosanna Redhill, the girl I rescued from the bar fire, runs this New Age shop called Mystique. She carries books on witchcraft and voodoo, ingredients for magic spells, crap like that. Her grandmother was a witch doctor." He explained about her past. "She actually tried to convince me that our arsonist is some kind of freak who can start fires with his hands."

Parker's eyelids twitched again. This time his eyes slid open, although they looked dazed, disoriented. Probably the pain or meds.

Or maybe he was warning Bradford to write the woman off as a kook and solve the damn case. But what if she had something to do with the fires?

He didn't think so, and his instincts usually were right.

Another possibility teased the back of his mind, one he couldn't dismiss. She had been present at three of the fires. And she had known two of the victims.

What if someone really was targeting her, and had meant to hurt her?

Just because she didn't know who it was,

didn't mean she didn't have a stalker. He could be a stranger, someone she'd barely met who'd developed an obsession with her...

Chapter Nine

Rosanna was shaken by the detective's reaction and battled tears all the way to her shop. She'd been ridiculed before, but for some reason Bradford Walsh's opinion cut her to the bone.

Did he really believe she was capable of starting the fires to get attention? That she was crazy…

Maybe she *was* letting her imagination get away from her. Maybe the fires had been simple acts of vandalism, or some form of gang initiation. Or perhaps a new group like the Santeria cult that her grandmother had spoken of when Rosanna was little had congregated in the area.

Maybe he would find the answers without her assistance, and she'd never have to see him again.

She choked on a sob, parked in back of her store and hurried inside. The scents of the candles, herbs and roots in the store filled her nostrils, soothing her nerves. Yet the books on magic and voodoo mocked her from the shelves.

Maybe the fires *had* been started by another form of magic, not someone possessing firestarting abilities. Someone could have concocted a spell or read one from a book or off the Internet. She even carried items in her store that could be used to create a potion.

Driven to find the answer, she spent the rest of the afternoon and evening in the shop reading about voodoo, witchcraft practices, magic and paranormal phenomenon in between helping customers.

According to her research, many magicians believed that magic came from a person's will, and involved the knowledge of power over evil. She found magic spells for both good and evil. Spells on how to make a man fall in love with you, protective spells for your house and family, ridding a place of evil spirits, as well as spells for medical practices like curing a disease, easing a headache, caring for a burn and reversing the aging process.

Others were more disturbing. One voodoo spell could make you go insane, and another would put live things like snakes, frogs or worms inside your body. Burning black candles, photographs, graveyard dust and coffins were used to make someone go away.

The dreary hot temperature seemed to drive customers inside, ensuring she had a steady business all day. By the time she closed the store, her head was spinning. The detective would think the reading material complete fiction, but since she'd learned that the origins were based in spirituality, and witnessed the way her grandmother had saved countless people, even reversed what they thought were tricks and spells cast upon them, she found the books fascinating.

Thunder rumbled outside, the threat of rain a welcome reprieve from the insufferable humidity. Anxious to get home in case a storm hit, she locked the door, closed down the register and tidied the store. Exhausted, she walked over to the front display windows to pull the shades, but the hair on her arms suddenly stood on end.

The feeling of being watched returned, and she glanced through the window, her heart hammering when she noticed someone standing in the shadows of the awning. She couldn't see his face, only the silhouette of a tall dark frame hunched against the corner.

Then suddenly one of the candles in the window display lit up.

She gasped, then took a step backward when the wick of another one flamed up. One by one, the row of candles adorning the table came alive, their yellow flames flickering against the darkness.

She glanced through the window again and started to rush to the door, to call to the stranger, but he disappeared into the shadows around the corner. For a miniscule of a second she considered chasing after him, but that would be stupid.

If he was dangerous or had started the fires, what would he do to her if she caught him?

WHEN BRADFORD arrived at the station, Captain Black called a meeting to discuss the investigation. Bradford reported on Parker's condition—he had been taken off the critical list and was stable now, although he still wasn't cognizant enough to discuss the fire—then explained about the fire at the cemetery. He didn't have the CSI report in hand but would follow up.

"We found two guys present at the bar with police records," Detective Fox stated. "I'm checking them out this afternoon."

"What kind of rap sheets?" Bradford asked.

"Silas Meters is twenty and was arrested for vandalism in his teens. Nothing lately, but who knows?" Fox consulted his notes. "And we traced Dugan Glacier to a local gang. They're into drugs, gangbanging, violence."

"Sounds like two viable leads," Black said. "Walsh, I want you to do some research, see what you can find nationwide on arsonists. Maybe we have a guy who relocated from another city."

Bradford nodded. "I'm on it."

Determined to find concrete evidence and a suspect, Bradford spent the afternoon researching databases for similar cases across the country.

A global search on arsonists with prior

convictions, especially paroles recently released, turned up two names in the southeast area. Barry Coker and Stuart Lumpkin. Only according to the police reports, the men's MOs were different than their current UNSUB. Coker used gasoline while Lumpkin preferred handmade explosives.

But Bradford would check them out anyway. If one of these felons had resurfaced, he might have altered his MO to mislead the police.

Coker was released six months before and was living in South Georgia, in Vidalia.

Vidalia wasn't too far from Savannah.

The other man, Lumpkin, lived in the mountains of Tennessee.

Bradford placed calls to both men's parole officers, explaining the circumstances and asking them to locate the men, and have the locals check their alibis.

He checked the system again, and one more name appeared—Johnny Walsh, his little brother. Nineteen years old, serving time in the Atlanta Pen for burning down a juvenile facility last year, the same one where he'd been sent when he was fifteen to get his act together. Three kids' lives had been lost. Johnny was serving twenty-five to life.

If he was ever released he would be middle-aged. His youth would be gone. Career goals impossible.

Not that Johnny had had any career goals.

The familiar ache that assaulted him when he thought of his lost family nearly crippled him, but he forced himself back to the task at hand. He'd stopped Johnny from setting more fires and taking additional lives, and he had to stop this guy, too.

Erring on the safe side, he phoned the prison where Johnny was locked up and asked to speak to the warden. "Warden LaGrange, this is Detective Walsh. How's my brother?"

"You heard about the fire?"

Bradford clenched the phone with a white-knuckled grip. "What fire?"

"Your brother set one last week in his cell, and was injured. He's in the infirmary now. The doctors say he'll make it, but he suffered burns on his hands and face, and is bandaged and sedated now."

Bradford wheezed an anguished breath.

"I would have called you," the warden

continued, "but your brother stipulated that he wouldn't accept calls or visits from you, and that if anything happened to him, that you were not to be notified."

Bradford's gut twisted with mixed emotions. Johnny had finally been a victim of his own wrongdoings. It served him right, although pained Bradford to know that he was suffering.

And he knew his brother didn't want to see him. "Was Johnny trying to escape?"

"I don't know. It's possible, but Doc says it might have been a suicide attempt. We have him heavily guarded, and he's on medication, too."

Bradford contemplated a visit, but why bother? Johnny had made it clear that he didn't want to see him, that he hated him. "Does my mother know?"

"Yes, she visited him the day after it happened."

And she hadn't bothered to call and tell him. "Keep me posted on his condition." He thanked the warden, then hung up and rapped his knuckles on the scarred wooden desk in frustration.

It did no good to stew over his family,

though, so he ran another search, this time narrowing the scope by specifying arson cases in which no accelerant had been discovered. Maybe their UNSUB had discovered something that was untraceable.

It took several minutes for the program to process his request, and he grabbed a cup of bad coffee while he waited, slugging it down. Finally he had a hit.

A case in Salem, Massachusetts, four years ago where an arsonist named Manny Blunt targeted modern-day women practicing witchcraft. He had trapped the women, tied them to a stake and burned them to death, claiming that he was following the footsteps of his long-dead ancestors who'd participated in the original Salem witch trials.

Blunt's first kill had been his mother. According to him, she was a witch who'd cursed his father and made his dick shrivel up and fall off.

Bradford chuckled. Psycho.

Still, the man's motive made him think of Rosanna and her bizarre theory about paranormal activities. Her grandmother had practiced as a witch doctor.

Did Rosanna practice witchcraft? Had her friend Natalie?

He crushed the foam cup in his hand and tossed it into the trash. He didn't honestly think this arsonist was targeting women practicing witchcraft, did he?

Unless Blunt had developed a fan club while in prison. It wouldn't be the first time a serial killer had earned a groupie.

He studied the pictures of the burned women from Blunt's file and compared them to the bar scene.

Blunt's victims had been tied to a stake and set ablaze for personal reasons whereas the bar fire appeared to be impersonal, a thrill kill. This arsonist could have killed hundreds, not just Natalie and the waiter.

Still, he'd look further into Blunt. He called and requested that records of the man's visitors and cell mates be faxed over, then ran a background check on him but discovered he had no family. He put in a call to the warden to get one of their officers to question him.

But as he hung up, he felt it was a dead lead. Maybe this latest killer wanted to cover his tracks and throw off the police by making it seem like he'd set the fire for excitement, not targeting a specific individual.

He leaned back in the chair, contemplating all the what-ifs. Rosanna and Natalie were the only common denominators between the fires at Cozy's and the Pink Martini. Rosanna had also known Terrance Shaver.

More and more he was beginning to believe that Rosanna might be a victim, and that she needed protecting.

DISTURBED by the candles suddenly erupting into flames, Rosanna blew them out, then examined the wicks and packaging to see if there was anything unusual about the candles. But she found nothing.

Worried they might be defective, she carried them to the kitchen in the back of her store, placed them inside the sink and wet the wicks. After being lit, she couldn't sell them anyway.

On second thought, she packed them in a bag and took them home with her. Then she could watch them and see if the oddity occurred again.

Exhausted from the trying day, she forced

herself to eat a salad, then showered and slipped on a cool cotton gown. She had just poured herself a small glass of Riesling when the doorbell rang. Startled at having company, especially so late, she checked the peephole and was shocked to see Bradford Walsh standing on her stoop.

Maybe he'd solved the case and had come to tell her they had the arsonist behind bars. Then she would never have to see him again.

Or maybe he was sending the men in the little white suits to get her.

Barely controlling a shiver of fear, she opened the door. His dark eyes skated over her, from her damp curly hair to her breasts, making her nipples tighten beneath the paper-thin gown. Even her bare toes, which she'd painted a kiss-me red tingled when his gaze found them. Suddenly realizing she wasn't wearing a robe, she folded her arms across her breasts. "I wasn't expecting you."

"I'm sorry," he said in a gruff voice. "I should have called first."

Her cat loped from the sofa to rub against her feet.

"I should have figured you'd have a black cat," he said with an edge to his voice.

"What is that supposed to mean?" she asked, her defenses rising.

He hesitated, then gave a quick shake of his head. "Nothing, I'm more of a dog person myself."

Her heart spasmed. "I had a dog once, a long time ago." In fact, she'd saved Doodlebug after her father died, but had lost the animal to old age when she was a teenager. She hadn't had the heart to replace him with another puppy. Instead her grandmother's cat had filled the void in her lonely life.

Not willing to elaborate, though, she asked, "Did you need something?"

The look he gave her sent a frisson of hunger through her. "Can I come in?"

She bit down on her lower lip, then nodded. "I suppose so. Let me grab a robe."

"Good idea," he muttered as he jammed his hands inside the pockets of his slacks. He was still wearing the dress shirt and khakis he'd worn to Natalie's funeral.

That thought sobered her as she dragged on a short robe and poked her feet into bedroom shoes.

When she returned to the den, he was studying the array of books on her shelf.

She cleared her throat, anxious to get this meeting over with. Her skin was tingling, her heart pounding. Remembering the earlier incident with the candles, she should be grateful for company. But Detective Walsh made her want something she couldn't have.

An honest, open relationship. One free of worries about some paranormal power that could be dangerous.

Judging from the scowl on his face, he didn't approve of her selection of reading material. "You have a lot of books on witch-craft," he said in a quiet voice.

She nodded. "As you know, my grand-mother believed in the magic of healing with herbs and homemade remedies."

"And spells?"

She shrugged. "Sometimes. The strength in believing can be powerful."

"What about you?" he asked, his expression hard. "Do you practice witchcraft?"

"No." She bit back further revelations. "Is that why you stopped by? To ask me if I practice witchcraft?"

"Yes."

His answer shocked her. "Why?"

His eyebrows slid upward. "How about your friend Natalie? Was she into witch-craft?"

"As a matter of fact, she dabbled in it, but she wasn't very experienced." She moved closer to him, wondering where he was heading with his questioning. "Now, tell me the reason for this inquisition."

His mouth twisted sideways. "I was re-searching arsonist cases across the States, and found one in Massachusetts where the perp targeted women practicing witchcraft."

His words sent a shiver of alarm through her, resurrecting painful childhood memories. Her grandmother had helped many people, but she'd been despised and feared by others. Some had vandalized her house, attacked her verbally and made physical threats. Rosanna had found dead animals in the yard, voodoo charms meant to turn the evil back on her grandmother.

"So you think this guy is here now, and that he targeted Natalie because she dabbled in spell-casting?"

He gave a clipped nod, looking wary. "No. He's still in the pen. But he might have a copycat, a follower imitating his crimes."

She had no idea what to say. The possibility was mind-boggling. But the censure in his eyes indicated that he thought her friend had brought trouble on herself by studying witchcraft. Maybe he thought she had, too.

"People have no right to judge," she said quickly, vehemently. "But even if you're right, how would someone know about my grandmother's practices, or that Natalie dabbled in witchcraft?"

"With the Internet these days, a smart criminal can find out personal information on anyone. Places you shop, your favorite dining spots and foods, items you purchase, vacation spots you prefer, movies you've rented." He angled his head toward the gris-gris in the shadowbox on her wall. "Did Natalie purchase items in your store?"

She nodded, sucking in a labored breath.

"Maybe he's been in your store, saw you and Natalie talking. Hell, he might have tapped into your files somehow, found names and addresses of buyers. Do you have a mailing list?"

She rubbed her hands up and down her arms, chilled at the thought of someone invading her privacy. "Yes."

"Credit card receipts can also offer personal information. So can Web searches, chat rooms you frequent…"

She waved a hand to stop him. "Okay, I get the picture." Stunned and trembling now, she sagged against the fireplace hearth. Shadow curled up by her feet as if to offer comfort, and she leaned over and rubbed his head, grateful for his unconditional love.

"I know it's a long shot, Rosanna," Detective Walsh said, "but right now I'm looking for any connections I can find. I reviewed the list of people at the café and bar, and you and Natalie were the only common denominator."

Disbelief mingled with fear in her chest. "So you think someone may have set the fire to kill us?"

"Like I said, it's a long shot, but I have to look into every angle."

His logic made the incident at her store stand out in her mind. "Someone was outside my store earlier, watching me," Rosanna whispered hoarsely.

"What? Why didn't you tell me this earlier?"

She shrugged, fatigue clawing at her. "I

don't know, I thought I was being paranoid. But after what you just said…it makes me wonder."

He gently gripped her arms then forced her to look at him. "Did you see his face, or recognize him?"

"No…" In her mind, she saw the candles lighting up one by one, flickering eerily against the night. The stranger's face watching her with that odd detached look, his eyes staring into the flames so intensely that he seemed enthralled by them.

A deep trembling started inside her and refused to release her from its hold. The past twenty-four hours had been too much. The fire at the café, then the bar. The trip to the hospital. Natalie's funeral. Terrance Shaver's death. The detective's accusations. His theory about the arsonist targeting witches.

The realization that she might have a stalker.

And her own theory—a man who could set fire with his hands, or maybe just his mind.

"I didn't mean to scare you," Detective Walsh's deep voice rumbled out soothingly.

Tears pooled in her eyes again, but she blinked them back furiously. She didn't know what to think, who to turn to, what to say. She was scared that he might be right, that this killer was after her.

But opening up to him terrified her more. Besides, he wouldn't believe her if she admitted the truth about her childhood.

What if this person knew about her gift? Knew about her past? Thought she was evil, a witch, like her father had.

Suddenly his eyes flickered with emotions that she couldn't read. She froze, the pain and panic in her chest squeezing her lungs so tightly she couldn't breathe. She'd never felt so alone in her life.

"I'm sorry, Rosanna, I didn't mean to upset you," he said quietly. "But I wanted you to be aware that you might be in danger, to be careful."

She shivered again, too stunned and confused to speak.

Then he stroked the hair away from her face, muttered a curse as if he was relenting to some temptation that he shouldn't. She felt the pull of his sexuality, the inde-scribable electricity between them.

His eyes darkened, then he shocked her by lowering his head toward her. Drawn to him, aching for comfort, she leaned forward.

A hiss left his mouth then he pressed his lips over hers and kissed her.

Chapter Ten

Bradford had no idea what possessed him to kiss Rosanna, but he couldn't stop. She was trembling, visibly afraid and shaken by his speculations, and she was grieving for her friend. She'd also suffered herself in the fire the night before. The close call with death must still be on her mind.

He shut out the voices in his head warning him that this was a mistake, that she might be unbalanced and manipulating him. But once he fused his hard, unforgiving mouth to her soft, supple, sweet lips, she tasted so enticing he couldn't release her. Her body felt oddly fragile while voluptuous at the same time, and it fit against his as if she was made to lie in his arms. Through the thin gown and robe, her nipples beaded to hard buds against his chest, fueling his desire, and he deepened the kiss, tasting and exploring her as his hands dug through that wild red hair.

A man could lose himself inside that riot of flaming curls.

A man could lose himself inside *her.*

She moaned softly, and raised one delicate hand and pressed it against his jaw. The yearning in that gesture, the subtle invitation for more, made his sex harden, and intensified his hunger to a burning need that threatened to consume him. He wanted to strip her gown, run his hands and tongue all over her tempting body and make love to her on the floor.

Hell, what was he doing? He hadn't felt this way about a woman in ages. Maybe ever. He'd always been in control.

The potency of his desire scared the crap out of him and jarred him back to reality. He broke the kiss, then stumbled backward and scrubbed his hand over his face. His breath whooshed out, harsh and labored in the deafening silence roaring through the room, while hers whispered toward him, enticing and soft, echoing with desire, tempting him to pull her back in his arms and feel it fan across his face.

He expected to see shock or anger, but her eyes looked dazed and cloudy with heat, and she clutched her arms over her breasts as if her body needed his touch just as his needed hers.

Dammit. He could not go there. Not with this woman. Not when she was involved in this case. Not when she might need saving, either from a killer or from herself.

He'd proven with his family that he was nobody's savior. Just a cop trying to do a job.

"I'm sorry," he said in a voice sharper than he intended. "I…don't know what got into me, but I promise it won't happen again."

She didn't say anything, just stared at him with those damned mesmerizing eyes, then licked those luscious lips. He swore he saw a smile fighting to surface on her mouth.

His own begged to taste her again.

Afraid he might give in to temptation again and lose all rational thought, he stormed out the door with a muttered goodbye.

ROSANNA LIFTED her fingers to her lips where they still tingled with pleasure from the detective's hot mouth on hers. She locked the door, then grabbed the glass of wine she'd poured earlier with shaking fingers, and sipped it, contemplating what had just transpired between them as she crawled beneath the covers. Shadow curled up on the foot of her bed, contented and sleepy, but in spite of the exhausting day, she couldn't relax.

Her body throbbed and ached with an emptiness she had never known, with one she didn't know how to fill. Only the man who'd awakened her desires could do that, and he had claimed the kiss was a mistake.

How could something that felt so incredible be wrong?

But he *was* wrong for her. He was obviously dead set against the idea of paranormal existence, which she could trace back to the very core of her ancestry.

Was that the reason he'd pulled away, or was it because he could tell she was inexperienced? Had he kissed her out of pity?

No, his reaction hadn't been pity. His body had hardened and throbbed against hers, and the electricity between them hadn't been one-sided.

Which confused her even more. She

didn't understand the detective. He didn't seem to like her or trust her, and she couldn't trust him with the truth, but she wanted him anyway.

Memories of being shunned at school and the brunt of neighborhood children's jokes because of her grandmother's shaman practices jarred her back to reality.

Maybe the study at CIRP would prove that she didn't possess a power, then she'd never have to reveal that part of her life. Maybe her father's death had been a freak accident, and she could stop blaming herself, or stop being afraid to get too close to other people for fear of hurting them.

Then maybe she could open herself up and explore the emotions mushrooming inside her every time the enigmatic man touched her.

Not that he would be interested. After he'd kissed her, he'd raced away as if fire was nipping at his heels. He didn't want any deeper involvement with her.

She had to accept that nothing would happen between them.

After all, neither one of her parents had loved her because she had evil inside.

How could anyone else love her now?

BRADFORD'S CELL phone rang as he drove toward Tybee Island. He checked the number, wondering if it might be Rosanna, but instead the display panel showed his captain's cell phone number.

He punched the connect button. "Walsh."

"Detective, one of our guys brought in something you should look at. It's a diary that belonged to Natalie Gorman."

"Where are you?"

"At the station."

"I'll be right there." He spun toward the precinct, grateful for duty to drag him from his own lust-driven thoughts. He'd never allowed emotions to distract him from a case before.

Well, except for his brother. And that had cost him dearly.

He wouldn't make that mistake again. Especially over a woman he barely knew.

So why did he want Rosanna Redhill so damn badly? Why had he considered going back and finishing what they'd begun with that kiss?

He was just horny, he decided. It had been ages since he'd bedded a woman. He'd have to remedy that one day soon, so his libido didn't interfere with another investigation.

A few minutes later, Bradford met Black in his office. He explained about the case in Massachusetts, and his chat with Rosanna.

"Interesting. Follow up on it," Black said. "That theory might fit with what I discovered about Natalie Gorman. Take a look at her journal and see what you think." He gestured toward the open book, and Bradford read the entry.

I think I'm a witch. I've been nervous about exploring it, but finally decided it's time. Today, I joined a research study at CIRP involving people with special abilities. I met a girl named Rosanna Redhill. She's kind of spooky but intriguing, and we became fast friends.

She owns a shop on River Street specializing in paranormal books and items. Tomorrow I'm going to her shop and buy some herbs and ingredients to test my spell making ability. I can't wait to see if I really have powers and what I can do with them.

"Did Miss Redhill tell you anything about this research study?" Black asked.

Bradford gritted his teeth. "No, sir, not a word." In fact, when he'd specifically asked if she practiced witchcraft, she'd denied it.

"Find out more about this experiment," Black said. "You can ask around at CIRP, although it's hell trying to get any information from them. Miss Redhill might be more helpful."

Bradford inwardly grimaced. He'd do whatever he had to do to solve the case. Even use Rosanna.

"You think this research project might have something to do with the fire?" Bradford asked.

Black shrugged. "That's what I want you to find out."

"You've been researching CIRP for a while?" Bradford asked.

"Yes. My wife, Sarah, was the god-daughter of one of the founders. She had a hearing impairment and received a cochlear implant there, but overheard a kidnapping plot and helped us track down a scientist they were forcing to work for them." Black paused. "Fox also investigated them, but they discovered his identity and performed a memory transplant on him to cover up a murder. He almost died."

Bradford muttered a curse.

"We're also working in conjunction with the feds to investigate Nighthawk Island. The center houses secret government-sanctioned projects. Most are highly classified, some involving nuclear and chemical warfare. Although the projects are cutting edge and may further medicine and science, occasionally one of the researchers crosses the line. One of the agents actually discovered a project where the scientists brainwashed children to become assassins."

Sweat beaded on Bradford's forehead. "My God."

"Yeah, and a few months ago, we learned about a twin identity experiment where one twin was kept against her will, drugged and received treatments to alter her identity."

"So you think an experiment might have something to do with our arsonist?" Bradford asked.

"I don't know, but the fact that Miss Gorman and Miss Redhill are both involved in it, and tied to our arson case, seems too co-incidental."

Coincidences lended to suspicion in Bradford's book as well.

He gritted his teeth. He'd question Rosanna without succumbing to this ridiculous lust eating at him. Remembering that she'd lied to him would keep him on track. Remembering her penchant toward the paranormal would be the clincher.

Once he'd listened to another woman who claimed she had special powers, the gift of second sight. But she led him astray from finding a missing child in time.

He'd never let that happen again. He'd lost that kid. Lost his family. Work was all he had.

And he wouldn't jeopardize it for anyone.

Not even if Rosanna's kiss and the taste of her sweetness haunted him for the rest of his life.

ROSANNA KICKED off the covers in her sleep. She was sweating profusely, so hot she thought she might die. Her skin prickled, felt sensitive, as if someone had lit up her body with a match and turned it into a burning inferno of need.

Bradford Walsh.

His lips caressed hers, his tongue danced inside her mouth, teasing her with promises of a wild night in bed and pleasure beyond anything she could imagine. Hands and bodies mated as he spread tantalizing kisses over her nipples, down her belly and between her thighs.

The pressure, the need, the heat was unbearable. Moisture dampened her center, and a raw ache drove her to press her legs together and roll to her side.

Then he was gone, and she was alone. The emptiness made her feel hollow, needy, and she pleaded for him to come back. To hold her and make everything all right.

To dip his tongue inside her mouth and trail his fingers along her spine. To strip her gown and stroke her sensitive skin. To love her with his tongue and hands until he made her his.

Rosanna jerked awake, on fire with need but suddenly chilled. The past two days' events rolled through her mind and grief choked her. Bradford's quick dismissal of their kiss added to her misery.

The air changed. Vibrated. Someone was in her bedroom.

Detective Walsh?

Maybe he felt the same desperate hunger that she did and had returned.

She didn't realize she'd called his name aloud, until the chill that had awakened her rifled through her again. Her skin beaded with goose bumps, and anxiety danced along her nerve endings. The window rattled, and thunder rumbled outside.

Whispers of another person nearby, an intruder, settled along her spine.

She swallowed hard and opened her eyes, searching the dark confines of the room.

One by one the candles she'd brought home flickered to life again and lit the darkness. The scent of vanilla filled the air, then cinnamon and roses. Then a masculine odor. Sweat. Cigarette smoke.

Her breath caught painfully in her chest and she sat up, searching the room. Shadow hissed and leaped from the bed and ran toward the door, with a yowl.

An intruder was inside her home.

Remembering Detective Walsh's statement about an arsonist burning women who practiced witchcraft, she reached for the phone to call for help.

But more flames shot up around her quickly, and she jerked her hand back to keep from getting burned.

Then the fire rippled around her bed in a wide arc just as it had Natalie's grave.

HE SMILED into the darkness as the candles lit a fiery halo around Rosanna Redhill's bed. She had sensed someone was in her bedroom, but she'd been too late to stop him. A brush of his hands across the tops of the candles, and his heat had transferred to the wicks. Her cat had hissed at him and he'd thrown a fireball toward it, laughing as the animal snarled and shot beneath the bed. Then he'd faded into the shadow of the doorway and focused all his energy and power into the cosmic force of nature that propelled that energy into more heat.

Heat that eventually seared the candle's wick and burst forth like a lightning strike sent by God.

That was what he had become—a god of fire, controlling part of the universe. Taking lives of the evil ones.

Following his destiny.

Just as Rosanna would follow hers when she died.

He dropped another fireball into the doorway then another on the steps as his final goodbye present.

He couldn't wait to see Brad boy's face when he saw Rosanna Redhill burning alive…

Chapter Eleven

Anger surged through Bradford as he left the police station. Rosanna hadn't met Natalie at her store, but at CIRP during a research experiment involving paranormal powers.

Why hadn't she told him the truth?

Because she'd known what his reaction would be? Because the experiments teetered on the unethical side like others had at CIRP? Because they were enhanced with some new illegal drug their scientists were researching?

Or could she possibly know the firestarter and want to protect him?

She would tell him the truth.

But not tonight. Not when he was still taunted by that kiss.

Besides, she'd been exhausted and fragile,

and grief-stricken when he'd left her. She needed rest, and he needed time to wrangle in his sex-starved craving.

He'd been a fool to try to comfort her and believe that he could stop at that. Touching her meant that spurt of sexual energy that he'd felt the first time he'd laid eyes on her had erupted to life.

He'd kissed the hell out of her. One more minute, one more moan and he'd have had her clothes off and his mouth on her body. One taste of her flesh, and he'd have been inside her.

Another bout of anger added to his turbulent emotions. Anger at himself for his loss of control, for forgetting that as a cop he couldn't allow emotions to enter the picture and distract him. Because he couldn't trust anyone.

His family had taught him that, and his job had long cemented it into his brain.

His cell phone jangled, and he snapped it up, quickly checking the display panel. Black.

He connected the call. "Walsh."

"Detective, a 9-1-1 call just came in from Rosanna Redhill. Her apartment is on fire."

Damn. "I'm on my way." He spun around and raced toward her place, grateful traffic tonight wasn't as thick as it had been on the Fourth. Still, tourists crowded the area, making the drive torturous.

The wail of sirens rent the air, and by the time he reached Rosanna's, fire was shooting up into the sky from the second floor. Her bedroom most likely.

Panic squeezed the air from his lungs.

Had she escaped or was she trapped inside again?

ROSANNA DROPPED the phone onto the bed, then tried to beat the flames with her pillow, but she wasn't fast enough. They snapped and hissed, clawing at the bedskirt and rippling upward to eat at the quilt. The scent of burning fabric and wood nearly choked her as she leaped over them. Fighting panic she ran toward the door but flames consumed it.

She grabbed a pillow to stuff over her mouth to keep from inhaling too much smoke, and peered through the thick plumes to see if the rest of the apartment was on fire. If she wrapped herself in a blanket, maybe she could run through the flames and make it downstairs. She had to find Shadow and take him with her or he would die. She couldn't lose him; he was the only family she had left.

But she spotted flames darting toward the ceiling in the hall and on the staircase and Shadow was nowhere in sight.

Oh God. She couldn't escape down the stairs.

Her childhood flashed back. The pitiful few dates and relationships she'd tried to have in college. The last two years of being lonely.

She didn't want to be alone forever, or to die and never have been with a man.

No time to think, though. She had to find a way out. Sirens roared in the distance, then grew nearer. Would they reach her in time?

The fire was spreading like a rabid beast eating up her four-poster bed now, and heading toward the curtains. Heat scalded her face, arms and feet as she jumped over the patches of flames and rushed to the bedroom window.

She yanked the curtains aside, then jerked up the blinds, unlocked the window and pushed at it, but the window was stuck.

Sweat trickled down her arms, and flames hissed at her feet as she shoved and struggled. Her eyes stung from smoke and tears, and she screamed in frustration.

Whoever had painted the room had painted the window shut.

Her heart pounding, she ran into the bathroom, grabbed a towel, wrapped it around her fist and rammed it into the glass. The pane shattered, sending glass pelting through the air. She broke another pane, then another, then looked down. No fire escape.

"Shadow!" she called the cat's name over and over, scanned the room, checked the closet. But she didn't see him anywhere. Maybe he'd made it down the steps.

Desperate, she ran back to the window and tried to judge the distance to the ground. If she jumped, she'd probably end up killing herself.

But if she didn't, the fire would eat her alive.

BRADFORD'S CHEST tightened as he threw the car into park and ran toward Rosanna's. The fire truck arrived at the same time, roaring to a stop, the firefighters jumping into motion. He identified himself as they began unrolling the hose and dousing the outside of the house where flames shot up. "The woman who lives here called it in," Bradford said. "She may still be inside."

He headed toward the door to check for her, but they stopped him with an out-stretched hand.

"I have to save her," he barked.

"We'll get her out." Before he could argue, two firemen raced inside to check the interior.

Feeling helpless for the second time in two days, he circled the house to see if the entire apartment was on fire. Smoke curled toward the sky, rolling above the top of the house. Wood hissed and popped, sparks flying. But so far, the flames appeared to be contained on the second floor and hadn't spread to the adjoining apartment.

His heart pounded when he spotted Rosanna hovering at the edge of one of the windows. She leaned through the opening, gasping for air, then stared at the ground as if she was contemplating jumping.

"Rosanna, wait!" he yelled.

She reached for the windowsill, and he panicked. She hadn't heard him.

He shouted again, waving his arms frantically. "Rosanna, wait, I'll get help!"

She spotted him, her eyes wide with terror. "Help me! I can't get out!"

"Hang on, I'll get a ladder!" Blood pounded through his veins as he raced around the side of the house to the front, and he grabbed one of the firefighters. "The woman's at a back window. I need a ladder!"

The firefighter nodded, grabbed a ladder from the truck and followed Bradford around back. Smoke flowed through the window now, and soot stained Rosanna's face as she hung her head through the opening, gasping for air.

He wanted to climb up and get her himself, but the fireman shoved the ladder against the house, then rushed up the steps. Bradford clenched his hands into fists as Rosanna climbed through the window, clutching the firefighter's hand, and leaning on him as he helped her down to safety. As soon as her feet hit the ground, he caught her arm and pulled her against him.

Pale-faced, she was shaking and crying. "My cat, Shadow, my cat! He's still in there."

"Rosanna…" He rubbed her arms, hating the anguish in her voice.

"Please, he's all I have left. He belonged to my grandmother."

She looked so tortured, he made a snap decision. "Get her to the paramedic," he ordered the firefighter.

Then he turned and raced up the ladder. He had to find that damn cat and bring it back to Rosanna. She yelled after him and so did the firefighter, but he quickly climbed the steps, took a deep breath and peered through the window.

"Shadow!" He scanned the patches of flames, the dark room, and suddenly the cat leaped from the corner, clawing at the curtains. "Here, kitty." He reached out a tentative hand, dropped inside the window and stooped to call him. "Come here, buddy, I'm going to get you down, take you to Rosanna."

He thought the cat might attack him, but he lowered his voice again, putting out his hand and coaxing the animal toward him. Finally the feline climbed into his hands, and Bradford pulled them both through the window. Flames nipped at his heels, and the wardrobe crashed and splintered behind him.

He was breathing hard by the time he reached the bottom and raced around front to the ambulance.

Rosanna was sitting on the stretcher with an oxygen mask, but the minute she saw him she dropped it and held out her arms. Tears streamed down her face as he placed the animal in her lap. She buried her head against the cat's fur, stroking him and crying.

Neighbors had gathered on the sidewalk to watch, some still in their pajamas. The fireman retrieved a blanket from their emergency supply, shoved it toward Bradford,

"Are you hurt, miss?" he asked.

She shook her head, and he nodded, then rushed away to help contain the blaze.

Bradford settled the blanket around Rosanna's shoulders "Are you really all right, Rosanna? Do you need a doctor?"

"I'm okay," she whispered. But her face looked ashen as she angled her head and watched the blaze destroying her home. He couldn't shake the emotions tightening his chest—this fire had nearly taken her life, just as the other one had killed her friend Natalie.

Unable to help himself, he hugged her tighter.

"Are you sure you're okay?"

She burrowed into his arms, and he kissed her hair, grateful she'd survived.

"Someone was in my house earlier," she whispered in a haunted voice.

"What?" He pulled back, searched her face, saw the conviction in her eyes. "Did you see an intruder?"

"No, but I smelled cigarette smoke and sweat—" Her voice broke. "Then the fire broke out."

He grimaced. If she was right, and someone had intentionally set the fire, they'd obviously meant to kill her.

And if he and the rescue workers had been five minutes later, the man would have succeeded.

ROSANNA CLUTCHED her cat, and hovered in the detective's strong arms, unable to tear herself away from his embrace. She felt safe as long as he was holding her, yet she couldn't banish the images of the fire hissing at her feet ready to eat her alive. And the realization that a stranger had been inside her house.

A stranger who'd tried to burn her apartment down and kill her.

But why would someone want her dead?

She didn't have any enemies. Not that she knew of anyway.

What if the detective had been right, and this maniac arsonist was targeting women he thought practiced witchcraft? If he was the same man who'd been outside her shop and made those candles burst into flames, then he knew about her business. And he obviously knew where she lived.

Maybe he even knew about the research experiment.

Could he possibly be part of it?

Embarrassed at her emotional outburst, and the way she was clinging to him, she wiped away her tears and pieced her composure back together. She'd always stood alone, and she always would.

But as she pulled back, she suddenly felt bereft, empty inside, as if she'd lost something precious that she'd almost had within her grasp.

Ridiculous. How could she miss something she'd never had?

He cleared his throat. "Rosanna, are you sure you don't need a doctor?"

"Yes." She gripped his arm, alarming

Shadow whose ears perked up as he prepared to protect her. "The last place I want to go is to the hospital."

The detective's dark gaze latched with hers, and he nodded. Around them the fire-fighters continued to bark orders and worked to extinguish the blaze.

"Tell me what happened?" he asked gently.

She closed her eyes, weighed how much to tell him. Braced herself for his reaction as she tried to calm the cat. "I was in my apartment, and went to bed. I'd brought these candles home from the store."

"And you lit them?"

She tucked an errant strand of hair behind her ear. Smelled the lingering smoke and cringed. "No."

"So how did the fire get started?"

"It did start with the candles." She glanced up at him warily, saw the skepticism in his eyes and her stomach clenched. "You aren't going to believe me. I mean it's hard for me to believe it myself."

An impatient look tightened his face. "Try me."

She stewed over her reply, but in the end,

she had to be honest. "Whoever broke in set the candles on fire."

"You saw him do this?"

"No, but they just burst into flames around my bed just like the fire at Natalie's grave."

A long sigh filled with disdain rolled from his lips. "Rosanna…"

"I know you think I'm crazy or that I'm trying to get attention, but I'm not. It's difficult for me to tell you this because I know how narrow minded you are—"

"I am not narrow-minded," he snapped.

"You aren't open to the possibility of paranormal phenomenon?"

"I believe in concrete things I can see and prove," he argued. "That's how cops think. We have to have physical evidence to show to a judge, not talk of hocus-pocus."

"I understand, but I know what I saw," she said, pleading with him to believe her.

"So you expect me to tell the other officers and the fire chief what? That someone is setting fires with his mind?" He paced away from her, the air fraught with tension. "Dammit, Rosanna, if I did that, they'd put me in a straitjacket and cart me off to the funny farm."

She turned away, considered bolting. If he wouldn't believe her, she had no place to go.

She'd have to solve the mystery behind this firestarter, and find out why he wanted to kill her by herself.

BRADFORD STRUGGLED to hold on to his temper. Concern for Rosanna threatened to rob his logic. The thought of her dying in that fire resurrected every protective instinct he'd ever possessed.

But thankfully, his police training had kicked in when he'd heard her bizarre explanation.

Yet even as he did, the urge to pull her back into his arms and feel her breath against his neck, to assure himself that she was alive, tormented him. "Listen, Rosanna," he said in a low voice. "I will find out who tried to burn down your apartment tonight, But I'll do it with solid evidence."

She seemed to withdraw into her silence, but fear radiated through every breath she exhaled. Around them, the firefighters raced, the smoke billowed toward the sky, and the muffled spectators' curious questions mimicked his own.

Bradford moved through the crowd, asking if anyone had seen someone lurking around.

"No, no one," a gray-haired woman said, fanning her face. "Who do you think did this?"

"You think someone set the fire intentionally?" a young man asked.

"We don't know yet," Bradford said. "That's what I'm trying to determine."

A teenager with a nose ring piped up. "That's the spooky girl from Mystique. Maybe she was casting some spells."

Rosanna blanched.

Their suspicious, condemning looks raised his defenses, although he didn't understand the reason. Hadn't he contemplated the same possibility?

The head firefighter approached them, lifting his mask. "Ma'am, we have the blaze contained and the fire is dying out. We managed to save most of the downstairs, but I'm afraid smoke and water damage ruined your clothing and upstairs furniture."

He expected her to wilt beneath the announcement, but she jutted up her chin and nodded. "Thank you for saving what you could."

He nodded and pulled Bradford aside to discuss the cause of the fire.

Bradford explained Rosanna's assertion that an intruder had been inside, and the firefighter nodded. "Then we'll definitely treat this as arson."

A CSI team arrived, and Bradford told them to search for trace evidence of an accelerant, and to confiscate the candles Rosanna had mentioned, if anything remained of them, so they could analyze them in detail.

He hated to leave Rosanna alone for a second. Exhaustion lined her face, and a sadness darkened her eyes, one that tore at his gut.

In just two days she had lost a friend, most of her belongings and nearly died.

Twice.

Admiration for her mingled with sympathy. She was still fighting, pasting on a brave face, proving she had guts and stamina.

He filled the CSI team in on her story, suggested that because of Rosanna this fire might be related to the one at the Pink Martini where two deaths had occurred, emphasizing the importance of finding evidence of the perpetrator, then hurried back to Rosanna.

She was so quiet, so curled within herself that he feared she was going into shock.

He gently touched her arm. "Rosanna, we can go now. I'm going to take you to a hotel for the night."

Her gaze swung to his, startled. Uncertain. Afraid. But she allowed him to guide her to his car without a word.

Silently he warred with that decision as she cradled the cat in her lap and fastened the seat belt. A hotel would be the wise choice. Leave her alone so he could save his own sanity.

But her fragile state warned him that she needed to be watched. Didn't need to be alone. Hell, if she wasn't stable...

No, he couldn't desert her tonight. No one deserved that fate after her frightening ordeal.

His captain's words echoed in his head. He wanted Bradford to find out what was going on at CIRP. If the research project was related to the fire.

He needed to know why she'd lied to him about her first meeting with Natalie. Besides, it was his job to protect the citizens so watching her was strictly business.

But as she leaned against the passenger side of the vehicle and hugged the cat, he knew he was lying to himself. In spite of the case and her interest in the paranormal, he was starting to care for her. He even stopped at the store to buy her damn cat some food before he took her home with him for the night.

DAMN BRADFORD WALSH. He'd saved the woman…

He was always around, like a hawk that followed him everywhere he went.

And what was with Rosanna Redhill anyway? Was she some kind of cat with nine lives? She should have died in that fire. Should be lying amidst the blaze with the heat melting her features. With that red hair of hers crinkling as the flames turned the strands to a smoldering brown ash.

Where were they going now?

He'd have to follow and find out.

No, that might be too risky.

After all, he knew where she worked.

Knew she'd be at CIRP for the research project.

Breathing in the scent of charred wood, smoke and ash, he reined in his disappointment. Brad boy still had no idea what he was dealing with.

Meaning he had time to play some more.

Renewed heat spiraled through him, and he felt its power surging through his fingers. Laughing as the firefighters finished rolling up the firehose, and the crime scene unit began to search for evidence, trace materials they wouldn't find, he mentally began to plan his next glorious moment.

The people who'd been drawn from their homes to watch his latest handiwork, their faces etched in terror, slowly dispersed, heading back into their homes where they would wonder tonight if they were safe.

His breath quickened. No one in Savannah was safe. The thermometers were soaring. Record high temperatures would be recorded. Heat led to fire, which led to destruction.

His body stirred with arousal at the mere thought, his internal temperature rising.

He pictured all that heat smoldering,

growing hotter, more intense. So intense the sparks started flying.

Yes. Tomorrow was a new day, and he couldn't wait for it.

Chapter Twelve

ROSANNA FELT NUMB as the detective drove away from her house. She hated to leave her belongings, but it was too dangerous for her to go back inside tonight to try to retrieve anything. Tomorrow she could return and scrounge through the rooms to see if anything was salvageable. She'd need to file insurance forms, buy new clothes and toiletries and talk to the owner about renovations…

The tasks overwhelmed her.

At least you're alive, she reminded herself. Not like Natalie who hadn't had a chance to rebuild, to go on with her life.

But what kind of life was she going to have if someone kept trying to kill her?

The sights of Savannah passed in a blur, and she vaguely realized they'd crossed the bridge and were headed toward Tybee

Island. Marshland, small cottages, the scent of the ocean…everything whirred around her as if she were on the periphery, at a distance.

Five minutes later, the detective pulled into a clam-shelled driveway and parked in front of one of the small colonial style cottages. Marigolds splashed color along the front walkway while tall live oaks spun silvery Spanish moss around the edges of the property as if providing a secret hideaway.

"Where are we?" she asked.

"My place."

She gripped the door handle with one hand while stroking Shadow with the other. "I thought you were taking me to a hotel."

He turned to her, his husky presence filling the confines of the car. "You shouldn't be alone tonight, Rosanna."

She swallowed hard against the tears threatening to surface. "But I'm surprised you brought me here."

His eyes darkened. "You'll be safe with me tonight, and the arsonist won't know where you are. That's all that matters."

Safe? She shivered, not knowing if she'd ever feel safe again.

And who would keep her safe from falling for him?

A self-deprecating half smile flitted onto his face. "Don't worry, I promise I'll behave myself."

Meaning no more erotic kisses. "What if I don't want you to?" she asked softly.

His gaze met hers, and that strong, sexual draw pulled her toward him, a palpable force that grew stronger each second.

"You're vulnerable right now," he said in a husky voice. "It's natural to need comfort."

"Maybe," she conceded. "But what if it's more than that?"

"Rosanna—" His voice broke. "You're in danger, and I'm going to protect you. That's all this is. That's all it can be between us."

He was right. But for some reason, she wanted more. And she sensed that he wanted it, too.

But as he climbed out, she tried to squash any illusions. Bradford Walsh was an officer of the law. He was doing his job. Letting her spend the night was nothing personal.

Although that kiss taunted her, along with the memory of his arms around her. Need drove her mad as he guided her inside, showed her to the guest room and handed her towels and one of his shirts to sleep in. And tenderness swelled inside her as he opened a can of cat food and offered it to Shadow. Even her cat, who usually didn't take to strangers, had warmed up to the man. He should; Bradford had put himself in danger to rescue him.

Determined to erase the memory of her earlier ordeal, she showered and washed the smoke from her skin, but the entire time she bathed she imagined the detective's big, strong hands skating over her body, touching her sensitive places, erasing the pain of the past few days and replacing it with exquisite pleasure.

BRADFORD OPENED the patio door and inhaled the marshy scent and the salty sea air, keeping his libido in check, but images of Rosanna naked and wet, slippery with soap, steam floating around her voluptuous body, tormented him.

He'd never felt this incessant need for a woman before. And he had no illusions that his lust was anything but male hunger. No altruistic thoughts here, just the physical need for release, simple lust for a hot night between the sheets, with bodies grinding together, lips and tongues teasing and tasting and Rosanna moaning beneath him as he filled her.

His sex hardened and throbbed with the need for release, and he paced into the kitchen, grabbed a beer and walked outside to clear his head. Rosanna seemed uncomfortable when she'd first entered his cottage, but her cat had made himself at home, lapping up his food; he now lay curled in Bradford's recliner as if he owned the place.

Footsteps padding softly on the carpet alerted him to the fact that Rosanna had finished showering and was approaching. The whisper of sweet smelling shampoo and her body heat wafted toward him, and he closed his eyes, savoring her fragrance for a moment before he had to face her, and put on his detached mask.

He couldn't allow this relationship with Rosanna to get any more personal. Not and do his job.

She might have been through hell tonight, but she'd still lied to him, and he had to find out the reason.

"Detective?"

Dammit. Her voice was as soft as satin.

"You might as well call me Bradford." Wrapping his iron-clad control around him like a sheath, he turned to face her. A sliver of moonlight had broken through the dark, heavy clouds, and streaked her face, illuminating her wide, green eyes and accentuating her fragile state.

"Bradford?"

"Yes." He forced a deep breath, because the sight of her wearing nothing but his T-shirt with her hair damp and her skin glistening from the shower was almost more than he could bear. "Can I get you something to drink? Water. A beer? Glass of wine? A soda? Hot tea?"

A small smile played on her delicate lips. "You have hot tea?"

He chuckled. "Actually no. But I could go to the store."

"No, thanks. I'm hot enough already."

God. So was he.

A blush stained her pale cheeks as if she realized the underlying meaning. But the sultry look that followed shattered his restraint.

Tension rippled between them, and he forgot all reason. He closed the distance between them, and pulled her into his arms. With a sigh, he threaded his fingers into her long tresses and drove his mouth down on hers. The kiss was stormy, filled with want, desire, passion.

She arched her body, pressed her breasts into him and clutched his arms as if she might fall if he released her.

He *was* falling...falling for her quiet sweetness and vulnerability. For her heady taste and mesmerizing eyes and soul-stirring angelic voice.

He deepened the kiss, trailed his fingers along her shoulders, down her back, over her arms, pulling her closer against him, so close her nipples budded and teased him through the shirt, so close he dipped his head and tasted the slender column of her neck. His lips and hands moved of their own accord, gently stroking her, easing up the shirt, feathering over the satiny swell of her breasts. She made a small, throaty sound of need, and he lowered his mouth and kissed her neck, lapping her skin until his lips closed over one turgid nipple.

She scraped her hands down his arms and whispered, "Please don't stop."

His sex throbbed, so relentlessly he ground his hips against her wanting relief. Aching for more, he suckled her other breast, until he knew he had to have her.

Thunder rumbled, cracking the sky with its announcement of impending rain, and he suddenly realized what he was doing.

God help him he didn't want to stop.

But lightning tore through the sky, reminding him of the fire earlier, and the questions left unanswered.

He jerked himself away, hurriedly straightened the shirt. "I'm sorry—"

"Don't apologize," she said in a shaky voice. "We both wanted it."

Hurt and anger laced her voice, but the thready strains of unspent passion quivered there, too.

Only that want would have to go unsatisfied.

The wind picked up, hurling leaves and shells across the patio. Reminding himself that she had to explain the reason she'd lied to him, and find out more about the CIRP experiment, he ushered her inside.

When he faced her, he'd tacked his control back into place. Too bad his body hadn't caught up with his mind. Like a traitor, it still throbbed and ached, begging him to take her to bed.

ROSANNA WATCHED Bradford throw up walls again. Pull away.

Shaking from the intensity of her hunger, she crossed her arms and rubbed her hands up and down them. "Bradford…"

He held up a warning hand. "We have to talk."

"I don't want to talk about what happened," she said. "I just want you to hold me again, to kiss me and make me forget about the fire tonight."

"Rosanna, stop it. I'm trying to be professional." His voice dropped a decibel, hardened. Then he paced to the opposite side of the room in front of the small fireplace.

"I'll take that drink now," she said, needing something to calm her nerves. She'd never been bold enough to tell a man what she wanted before, and his rejection stung more than he could know.

He gave her a clipped nod, walked to the

adjoining kitchen, uncorked a bottle of merlot, poured her a glass and handed it to her.

"Thanks." She stared into the blood-red wine for a minute, humiliation streaking through her.

She wouldn't beg again. Or touch him.

Because touching him made her crazy.

She pivoted away from him, feeling lost and lonely as she stared out at the raindrops that began to pelt the patio and yard.

"It's peaceful here," she said softly.

"I thought it would be," he admitted. "But I haven't had time to take advantage of the beach the way I thought I would when I moved in."

"Maybe I should consider looking for a new place to live." She took another sip of the wine. "Depending on how much damage the fire did to my apartment, I may be displaced for a while…"

"You said someone was in your apartment. Can you remember seeing anything else? The intruder's face or eyes? How tall he was? Maybe a distinctive odor?"

She tilted her head sideways in thought. "No. I… it was more like I sensed him there.

And I did smell smoke, from a cigarette." A shudder visibly shook her body, as she relived the memory of the blaze.

"Are you sure you haven't crossed somebody, Rosanna? An old boyfriend or lover who might want revenge?"

"No. I…I haven't really dated anyone lately." In fact, she hadn't opened herself up to any man before.

So why did she want to open herself up to Bradford Walsh?

"Why did you lie to me about the way you met Natalie?"

She jerked her gaze to his, rattled by the question. "What makes you think I lied?"

His mouth thinned into a frown. "Because we found Natalie's journal at her apartment. In it, she said she met you at CIRP during a research project."

She inhaled sharply, questions tumbling through her mind. Just how much did he know?

"Tell me the truth," he said in a cold voice. "Why did you lie?"

She bit down on her lip, considered telling him everything. Maybe unloading the burden she'd carried all these years would finally free her and bring her peace.

But he'd rejected her earlier, had implied that she was crazy. If he knew the truth, he'd look at her with contempt.

Still, she had to tell him something. After all, he might already know the nature of the experiment.

"Rosanna, I can't keep you safe if you don't trust me."

She sighed. "I lied because you made it clear how you felt about paranormal activities. I saw the disapproval in your eyes when you visited my shop." Anger from her past resurfaced to tighten her voice. "I was ridiculed enough growing up to last me a lifetime."

"Because of your grandmother?"

"Yes."

"That must have made you angry."

Panic bloomed in her chest. "I learned to control my anger." Because she was afraid of it. Afraid that her anger made her evil, gave her the strength to do awful things.

She twisted her hands together. "What difference does it make how Natalie and I met?"

His dark eyes searched hers, as if daring her to lie again. "Because you and Natalie were both involved in that deadly fire, and you're both involved in the research project at CIRP."

She swallowed hard. "Terrance Shaver was a part of it, too," she admitted. "He claimed he could read minds."

His jaw tightened. "Why didn't you tell me this before?"

"I tried to tell you about the experiment at your office," she said bitterly. "But you told me I was crazy, then suggested I needed to see a psychiatrist."

Silence stretched between them.

Finally he spoke, his voice so calm that it was alarming. "So, Natalie, you and Terrance were all involved in the experiment. And you've all been targeted by this arsonist. Maybe this guy thinks you can recognize him."

She shivered and finished the wine, his declaration driving home the questions she'd asked herself earlier.

And the fear that she knew the firestarter personally.

"Rosanna, I'm going to need a list of all the people involved in the study."

"I don't know everyone's names," she said. "The scientists divided us into small groups. We only use first names, and everyone had to sign a confidentiality agreement to protect the identities of the participants."

He gave a clipped nod as if he wasn't surprised. Then he reached for the phone. "I'm going to request a search warrant to force them to give me the list."

She bit down on her lip, and studied the raindrops, fat ones now that plopped onto the brittle grass like teardrops. Her own silent tears fell, tears for all she'd lost, for the fear that kept her prisoner. For the relationships she could never have because of this cursed ability.

If he got the list, he'd probably learn why each of them had joined the study.

And if he dug deep enough, he might discover the rest of her secret. As a cop, he'd have to arrest her for murder and take her to jail.

Chapter Thirteen

Bradford studied Rosanna closely, anxiety riddling him as he placed the call. Captain Black assured him he'd work on the warrant overnight.

He hung up, and studied Rosanna again, noting the lines of tension tightening her mouth. She was holding back. He didn't know why, but instincts told him there was more to her story than she had admitted.

Her words echoed in his head—*I was ridiculed enough growing up to last me a lifetime.*

He tried to imagine what her life had been like. Witnessing her father's death at four years old. Growing up knowing that her mother had abandoned her.

Then being shipped to Savannah to live with an elderly grandmother who practiced witchcraft. A grandmother who most likely communed with other believers in the supernatural and paranormal.

She'd been ridiculed—by whom? Neighbors? Other kids at school?

How about the parents of those kids? Had they excluded her from birthday parties, and kept their children away from her because they feared her grandmother?

He pictured her as a reclusive kid, shy, a target for bullies, and his stomach churned.

But compassion for her had no place in the investigation. It would only blur lines that he had already tripped over when he'd kissed her. Lines that even now he was considering crossing again...

"Tell me about the research project," he said in an effort to steer things back on track.

She frowned. "You mean, you don't know what it's about?"

He shrugged. "I want to hear your version."

Releasing a shaky sigh, she walked over to the hearth and sat down on the edge. In spite of the wind whistling outside and the rain splattering against the roof, the room felt hot, the air cloying.

The scent of her filled his lungs. Intoxicating and painful because he couldn't act upon his craving.

"The project has been designed to study people who have some kind of paranormal ability. The basis is controlling mind over matter." She paused, and he waited, refusing to fill the silence, hoping she'd open up to him. The fact that he still wanted her, and that she didn't trust him bothered him more than he wanted to admit.

Finally his tactic worked.

"There are several small groups being studied," she continued, "along with another group that's being administered a drug the doctors think might stimulate mental energy and help in converting it to physical energy within the body."

He battled his skepticism over the possibility that such abilities existed, knowing that if he voiced that attitude now, she would clam up.

"You've met with the group?"

"Yes."

"Tell me about the participants."

Her sigh whispered out, riddled with anxiety. "We're in the early phases of meeting, but I don't think anyone in my group is the person you're looking for."

"Maybe, maybe not. But someone may have accessed the list. Or perhaps one of the subjects in another group saw you at the club and thinks you can identify him."

He had to dig deeper. "What kinds of abilities do the subjects claim to possess?"

"I really don't feel comfortable sharing this," she said softly.

"Why? Don't you trust me, Rosanna?"

"I told you we signed a confidentiality agreement."

"There's more to it than that."

She glanced into his eyes, and he saw pain, evidence of abuse perhaps. The ridicule she'd mentioned earlier.

God help him, he wanted to soothe her and erase her fears.

But he was not the man for that job. She needed, deserved, someone who had more to offer than a night of hot sex.

Someone who'd stick around and share her beliefs in this paranormal hogwash. Which he could never do.

"Rosanna?"

"One woman claims she dreams things

before they happen. Another lady communes with the dead. Terrance Shaver insisted that he was a mind reader."

Nothing he hadn't seen on TV.

He inched closer to her, struggled not to inhale her enticing scent. To remember that he was a detective trained in interrogation skills. "No firestarters in the group?"

She shook her head, then wet her lips with her tongue and looked up at him. Wariness and something else...desire...haunted her eyes. "No, but one man said he can freeze things with his hands."

Bradford clenched his hands by his sides, masking a reaction. Use her, his captain had said. Find out more about CIRP.

He reached out and feathered a strand of hair behind her ear. So delicate. So soft.

"What about you, Rosanna?" he asked in a low voice. "What kind of ability do you have?"

She wanted to trust him, he saw it in her eyes. She needed someone to believe her because she'd been shunned all her life.

He swallowed back bile, leaned close to her, so close his breath whispered in her ear. She shuddered against him, closed her eyes.

He forced his voice to a seductive pitch to keep her reeled on the line. "I know you're scared, Rosanna," he said softly. "But tell me, what ability do you have?"

BRADFORD'S seductive voice momentarily lulled Rosanna into wanting to share her deep-seated fear and secrets, that when she got angry she could move things with her mind. That she'd repressed her emotions all her life, terrified that she might hurt someone again if she lost her temper.

His breath brushed against her throat, and she inhaled the scent of rain and Bradford's masculine odor. He exuded raw power, strength, safety.

Yet he also threatened that safety by taunting her to lean on him. To trust him.

She'd never trusted anyone before. Trust led to hurt and hurt led to pain.

"What extraordinary ability do you have?" Bradford asked again.

She opened her eyes, remembered the torment from her childhood, the disapproval in his expression when she'd first mentioned the possibility of paranormal powers.

If she did possess an ability, she'd repressed

it most of her life. She could continue to do so.

Then and only then could she have a normal life. A life with a chance at a relationship with him.

And she wanted that with every ounce of her being. Even if it was only a sexual relationship…

So she lied. "I don't have one," she said, injecting conviction into her tone. "Having grown up with a healer, I was curious about the study. And I thought it might be interesting to share what I learned with people who frequent my store."

His eyes flickered over her, intense, scrutinizing. "Is that the only reason? You're not a healer like your grandmother?"

A sardonic laugh escaped her. "No, I'm definitely not a healer."

This time his expression registered acceptance. Maybe relief.

It was a step in the right direction.

Still, he'd go to CIRP tomorrow. Talk to the doctors.

But what could Dr. Klondike tell him about her? Nothing. After all, she had failed at her attempts to use telekinesis at the center.

And as long as she controlled her emotions, she didn't have to worry.

She started to reach for him, to cup his face in her hands and kiss him again, to feel the flames ignite between them, but he moved away from her, and gestured toward the guest room.

"We'd better get some sleep. Tomorrow I'm going to CIRP to question the doctors. If this arsonist is part of that experiment, I'm going to find the bastard and stop him before he can hurt anyone else."

She was tempted to ask him if she could sleep with him, but she'd never been that bold. If he said no, she couldn't handle another rejection.

And logic told her he would say no.

So she nodded and wrapped her arms around her waist as she walked into the bedroom alone.

BRADFORD WRESTLED with sleep all night, but images of Rosanna lying next door wearing nothing but his shirt kept him hard and edgy, and itching to join her in bed.

When he'd finally dozed, he'd kept one ear alert, listening for any sign that the arsonist might have followed them and launch another attack on Rosanna.

The next morning he shaved and showered in record time, then sipped coffee while he waited for Rosanna to dress. When she emerged from the guest room, she was wearing one of his shirts cinched at the waist by one of his ties, as a dress. Her bare legs were so sexy he had to look away.

He offered her coffee, and she accepted, the dark smudges beneath her eyes suggesting that she hadn't slept, either.

"You look tired," he said without thinking.

"Is that your way of telling me I look bad?" she asked without humor.

Hell, no. She'd look good if she was dead on her feet. "No. I'm sorry."

She shrugged, and he wanted to sweep her in his arms and make that frown disappear.

"I need to go by my apartment, see what might be salvageable. Find a place to stay. Get some new clothes."

"I'll drive you."

"Thanks,"

He offered her breakfast, but she declined. "I just want to get this day over with."

The conversation on the ride to her place

was stilted. In the early morning light, the strain on her face was evident in the vulnerable tilt to her chin.

The sight of the yellow crime scene tape encircling her home screamed of the night before. The invasion of a stranger in her life, the destruction of her personal belongings and her sense of security. The violence and realization that someone had intentionally tried to kill her.

That she still might be in danger.

"I'll go in with you," he offered.

"Thanks, but I'm a big girl. I can take care of myself."

Not against a killer, she couldn't.

He pressed a hand over hers. "Let me do this, Rosanna."

She hesitated, then nodded, gratitude shimmering in her eyes. But her face crumpled when she saw the extent of the damage as she toured the house. Most of the downstairs furniture could be refurbished, but the upstairs was in shambles. Smoke, fire and water damage had ruined the woodwork, furniture, her clothes.

"I'm sure this is overwhelming," he said, sympathy for her surfacing.

She pasted on a brave face that made his admiration rise a notch. "Things can be replaced."

"I'll call a service to clean up," he said. "But you may want to be here while they work so you can make sure they don't throw out something important."

She nodded, and he phoned to make the arrangements, then waited outside to guard the house and give her privacy until the crew arrived. He found her upstairs on her knees in the closet scrounging through a box of old photos. A sad smile curved her mouth as she traced a finger over a picture of an elderly woman. "I'm glad these pictures of my grandmother weren't destroyed," she whispered.

He squatted down beside her, slid a thumb beneath her chin and tilted her face up to him. "I need to go to the precinct, then out to the research park. Will you be all right?"

"Sure. I'm used to being alone."

"Where are you going from here?" he asked.

She sighed. "To talk to my landlord. Then shopping. I called Honey last night and asked her to open up Mystique today."

"You can reach me on my cell if you need me." He handed her a card with the police department's number and his personal cell phone listed.

"Don't worry about a place to sleep tonight," he said. "You're staying with me until this arsonist is caught."

Her eyes widened in shock, but he stood and left before she could ask why he wasn't doing the smart, logical, professional thing and taking her to a hotel.

He *should* do that.

But for more reasons than one, reasons he didn't want to pursue too deeply, he couldn't leave her alone tonight.

And he didn't trust anyone to keep her safe but him.

ROSANNA MANAGED to channel her emotions into energy as she sorted through the remains of her clothing and personal belongings. She had been honest when she said her clothes could be replaced. So could her jewelry, which was more trendy than expensive.

But the precious photographs of her and her grandmother were all she had left of their life together. That and her memories.

No one could steal those from her.

She had been the only person in Rosanna's life who'd truly loved her. An unconditional love.

And she had been a strange little child. Homely. Prone to telling stories about her grandmother's healing and incantations, which had frightened the other children.

Afraid to show emotions for fear of unleashing some power that might hurt others.

By noon, she'd salvaged what she could and boxed it up, then met with the landlord who looked distraught over the damage. He'd placed a call into his insurance company, and assured her they would get the repairs done as quickly as possible.

She grabbed some toiletries and left, then stopped by her favorite vintage shop and bought some new outfits.

After a light lunch at a nearby café, she checked in at the store, then headed to CIRP for her afternoon session, wondering what she would find. Had Bradford already gone to the center? Had he obtained the information he'd wanted?

Her nerves strung tight, she decided to snoop around on her own and see what she could learn. But if the arsonist belonged to the experimental group, she had to be careful.

Her stomach fluttered with anxiety when she passed the lab assistant in the hallway. He shot her an angry look, then she slipped into the room with the other telekinetic participants.

Dr. Salvadore addressed the group, "Today we're going to focus on relaxation techniques, tapping into our deep reservoir of power, and honing our individual skills." He gestured with his hands. "Remember we're working with energy we all possess, energy that gives us the ability to control mind over matter.

"Most people dwell on the negative things that happen in their life. Then those negative things actually happen, because you are actually drawing that negative energy toward you." The doctor paused, voice soothing. "Today rid yourself of those self-defeating thoughts and concentrate on positive energy. Choose something you want, whether it's money, fame, a lover. Visualize good things happening. Instead of moving the thing you want away from you, visualize moving it toward you. You see it within reach. Then see yourself holding it in your hands."

She proceeded to walk them through various exercises in positive thinking and visualizing success. Triggered by those suggestions, glimpses of images traipsed through Rosanna's mind—images of her and Bradford as a couple, of them solving the murder, making love, even ending up together forever.

She removed the button from her pocket, the one that had slipped off Bradford's shirt this morning. She planned to sew it back on, but now she used it for the experiment. She focused on the small object, on the energy in her body, on the attraction between her and Bradford. If she could move the button toward her, maybe she could somehow bridge the gap between them.

But her first attempts failed, and frustration knotted her shoulders. Still, she felt compelled to maintain a bottleneck on her emotions for fear of unleashing the evil within her that had erupted when her father had attacked her. And while she struggled to focus, she kept one eye on the others in the room, searching for someone who might be suspicious.

Someone who might have tried to kill her the night before.

Her lack of focus kept her from success again. Or maybe she didn't possess a telekinetic power after all.

Relief tugged at her. If she didn't have an ability, she wouldn't have to worry about hurting anyone or lying to Bradford.

As a wind-down to the session, the doctor walked them through several relaxation and deep breathing exercises. When she left the room, Rosanna scanned the labels on the doors as she walked down the corridor. Several doctors' offices flanked the hall, along with labs and administrative services. The man who'd claimed to freeze things stood staring at her from the lobby.

She darted into the rest room to calm herself, hoping he'd leave. Several minutes later, she held her breath as she ducked out the door. Thankfully he was gone.

Then she spied the door to the lab across the hall and poked her head inside. A nurse hovered at the desk, lost in conversation on the phone. She waited until the nurse turned toward the window, then hurried past and slipped back to the lab area.

Seconds later, she scrambled up to the computer, hoping to locate information on the study and the people involved.

She had just tapped into the file when a voice behind her broke the silence.

"What the hell are you doing?"

A guard appeared beside her, hand to his gun, shattering any hope she had of escaping.

Chapter Fourteen

Bradford hated to leave Rosanna alone to deal with the damage to her house, but he felt as if he was invading her privacy by watching her sift through her personal belongings. Besides, he had work to do.

He stopped by the precinct and met with the captain and other officers to discuss the case. He hoped that CSI had discovered some concrete evidence, but as in the other fires, they hadn't found traces of an accelerant. There had to be something they were missing, some new chemical that was undetectable through normal tests.

And the fax about Blunt and the interrogation notes from the warden at the prison didn't point to any groupie or copycat, at least none they'd discovered.

"We're still checking prints," the lead

CSI investigator said, "but we haven't found any except for the woman's and yours, Detective Walsh."

Dammit. "How about those candles?"

"They were melted, but preliminary tests on the wax and wicks indicate that they're normal candles that you could buy in any store in town."

Bradford relayed the nature of the research experiment at CIRP and received rolled eyes and grunts of skepticism.

"I don't think that chick's elevator stops on every floor," one officer muttered.

"You don't believe in that supernatural crap, do you?" another asked.

Captain Black gave him an odd look, and Bradford knew he was thinking about Bradford's past. That psychic and the botched assignment. And his brother…

"No, of course not," Bradford said vehemently.

"I still want you to investigate the project," Captain Black said. "It might be questionable. We know the doctors have utilized drugs in the experiment. Perhaps they've also used bionic parts or a computer chip that make it appear as if people have paranormal or superhuman abilities."

Good point, Bradford conceded. "Rosanna admitted that she knew Terrance Shaver, our last victim. And he's also part of the research project as was Natalie Gorman."

"Two dead and one attempted murder, all connected to CIRP," Black said. "It's definitely our best lead so far."

Bradford stood. "I'm going to pick up that warrant and talk to the staff now."

"Call if you need backup," Black said.

Bradford agreed, snagged the warrant, then drove to the research park on Skidaway Island. He first met with the director of CIRP, Dr. Ian Hall, and explained the reason for his visit.

The statuesque man leaned back in his leather chair with a worried look on his face. "I was sorry to hear about the deaths of those individuals, but I don't see how it relates to our work here. Since I've assumed leadership, I've worked hard to maintain the integrity of the scientists, staff members and the projects we undertake."

"I appreciate your position," Bradford

said, striving for diplomacy. "But two of the people involved in the same project have died as a result of arson, and another participant was almost killed in her home last night."

Dr. Hall chewed the inside of his cheek as if trying to decide his degree of cooperation. "We'll release the list if you give me your word that you'll keep our association out of the papers."

"Worried about bad publicity?"

"We've had our fair share of good and bad publicity, but my goal is to protect the privacy of our employees and patients."

"All right, for now. But if we discover that the arsonist is one of your staff members or that these crimes are directly related to a specific research experiment, that may not be the case."

Dr. Hall gave him a long assessing look, then finally nodded. "The experiment you're speaking of involves paranormal abilities."

Bradford handed Dr. Hall the warrant.

"The warrant is specific to the research study I mentioned," Bradford said, "so we won't be invading the privacy of participants in other projects."

The doctor examined it, then thanked him for keeping the warrant specific. Then he led him through the building to an office belonging to Dr. Klondike.

The sandy-haired physician narrowed her eyes at Bradford, her mouth flattening into a frown. "Our participants' privacy is at issue here," she argued. "We specifically had each person sign confidentiality agreements to protect them."

"We don't intend to advertise the details of the investigation," Bradford said, "but while you may be trying to protect the individuals' identities, I'm trying to save their lives." He produced files showing photos of the crime scenes, of Natalie Gorman lying on a slab in the morgue, of Terrance Shaver's burned corpse and the woman shuddered.

"Last night a third woman almost died. Actually she was also in the fire with Miss Gorman at the bar, but escaped." He paused. "I believe someone in the experiment may have set the fires and is afraid Miss Redhill might recognize him, so she's still in danger." He continued by explaining the profile of an arsonist who set fires for excitement, then ended by reminding her of the brutality of the deaths and the fact that the man wouldn't stop until he was apprehended.

"I just don't want us to lose credibility with our participants," the doctor said. "If people find out that we release names and personal information, they'll stop volunteering for our projects."

Bradford's patience snapped. "Maybe they should if it means they'll be murdered. And maybe you know the participant that fits this profile and are covering for him."

Dr. Klondike blanched. "I resent that suggestion."

"How long have you worked on this project?" Bradford asked. "Months? Years? I'm sure you don't want your experiment ruined, exposed."

The truth of his statement registered in the way the doctor averted her gaze.

"Do you know who's setting these fires?"

She shot an angry gaze his way. "No."

"If you do, you're covering for a murderer, and can be tried as an accessory."

Dr. Hall cleared his throat. "We have nothing to hide. Turn over the information, Dr. Klondike." Dr. Hall turned to Bradford.

"Just remember our agreement, Detective. You won't mention our research experiment to the press."

Bradford gave a clipped nod.

Dr. Hall excused himself, while Dr. Klondike reluctantly printed the information. Bradford's cell phone rang.

"Detective Walsh."

"It's Fox. We found that Georgia parolee, Coker, and are bringing him in for questioning. Thought you might want to be here for the interrogation."

"I do. See you shortly." He accepted the printout from the doctor, then headed to his car. Maybe they had their killer in custody already, and they'd get a confession.

Then Rosanna would be safe from the killer.

And he would be safe from her.

ROSANNA'S MIND whirred as she struggled to think of a plausible reason she might try to hack into the research park's computer.

"What is your name, ma'am?" the security guard asked.

"Rosanna Redhill," she said, then hesitated, realizing she should have made up a fake name.

"What are you doing here?"

"I belong to one of the research projects," she said, suddenly nauseous from the scent of antiseptic and blood in the room. Or maybe her nerves were causing the reaction. "I wanted to talk to one of the lab techs about my bloodwork from my last visit."

"There's obviously no one in here now. They've stepped out." He made a point of glancing around with a scowl. "Why were you touching the computer?"

She gathered her purse. "I was just fiddling while I waited… Thought I might check my e-mail."

"Our patient files and their labwork are strictly confidential. No one is allowed to use the computers without authorization," the security officer said. "You have no business being in here by yourself." He reached for his radio and she realized he was going to turn her in.

She backed toward the door. "I'm sorry. Actually I really thought Louis might be here. He and I are friends and…well, I just wanted to pop in and say hey to him." She shrugged, letting her smile suggest that she was involved with the lab guy who'd asked her out.

He relaxed his stance, then flipped a button on his radio and reported how he'd found her. She twisted her hands together while she waited to see what he intended to do with her. Arrest her?

He spoke quietly into the radio for several seconds, then must have connected to Dr. Klondike. Finally he angled his head toward her. "Dr. Klondike vouched for you. She wants to see you."

Dread mounted in her stomach as he latched a beefy hand around her arm and hauled her through the door.

But as she stepped into the hallway, she saw Louis duck into another doorway.

He'd been watching, had overheard her conversation with the guard. And the sharp anger that flared in his eyes indicated he knew she'd been lying. That anger made her rethink her initial impression of him. She'd first thought him gangly and odd, but shy and harmless.

Now the ominous look in his eyes suggested he could be violent.

Bradford had asked her if she had an old boyfriend who might be mad and want to hurt her. Louis had been at Natalie's funeral. She tried to remember if she'd seen him at the café or the bar. It had been so dark and crowded he could have been inside without being noticed.

No. Surely Louis wouldn't try to kill her just because she'd blown him off.

Would he?

BRADFORD MET Detective Fox at the station and joined him to question Coker in the interrogation room while their captain watched through the two-way mirror.

"We hear you're on parole," Fox began.

Coker, a ruddy-faced, big-bellied man with tobacco-stained teeth folded his tree-trunk arms across his chest. "Yep. Paid my debt to society. I'm free and clear. So why are you hassling me?"

Bradford cut to the chase. One by one, he listed the dates of the fires—first the cottage, the coffee shop, the bar, the car and then Rosanna's house, each time asking Coker to explain his whereabouts.

"Listen," Coker barked, "you got no right to try to pin those on me."

Bradford slapped a picture of Natalie Gorman's corpse, along with the waiter who'd died in the bar fire, onto the wooden table. "These people died because of someone's sick game of arson. You like arson."

Coker's eyes widened. "But I never killed no one."

Bradford made a clicking sound with his teeth. "There's always a first. You've been sitting in that cell a long time. Bored. Looking for some excitement."

"Only excitement I wanted when I was paroled was between a woman's legs."

Bradford shoved his face into the man's. "Your kind doesn't suddenly stop getting a thrill from setting fires. Trust me, I know."

Fox dropped another photo into the mix, this one of Terrance Shaver. "He was fried to a crisp," Fox stated bluntly. "Now, tell us where you were or we'll slap your ass in a cell."

Coker's eyes bulged with panic. "No, no cell. Not again."

"Then you'd better start talking," Bradford muttered.

Coker stood and yanked at the belt loops of his jeans. "I think I need a lawyer."

Bradford crossed his arms. "Lawyer makes you look guilty."

"Hell, we all know that's not true," Coker sputtered. "You want to pin this on me, you'll invent some evidence and frame me."

Bradford grabbed the man by the neck of his shirt. "Listen to me, I want the truth. Locking up the wrong guy is not going to help me. The real killer would still be out there. And this guy will kill again if I don't stop him."

Fox shoved a legal pad in front of Coker. "Write down where you were and who you were with for each of the dates listed."

Coker flattened a hand over his ruddy face, then cursed. But a second later, he began to write.

He didn't have an alibi for the first two fires, but he swore he was in Vidalia with a woman he'd hooked up with the night of the bar fire. And the night before when Rosanna's apartment was set ablaze, he claimed he'd been at a club in South Georgia.

Bradford tapped the pad. "Write down the name of the bar, and the woman's name."

Coker complied, then shoved the pad away with a scarred thumb. "Now, let me get the hell out of here."

Bradford glared at him but didn't respond. Instead he continued to push the man. "Do you know a woman named Rosanna Redhill?"

A leer colored Coker's face. "No, why? Is she hot? Wanna set me up with her?"

Anger churned through Bradford at the thought of the man putting his grimy paws on Rosanna. "No. Someone set fire to her house last night while she was inside."

"I told you where I was…at that club in South Georgia." He leaned back and puffed out his cheeks. "I've cooperated, now let me go."

Fox reached for the door. "Not till we check out your story."

He and Bradford exchanged a look of agreement, then stopped outside. They'd let the ex-con sweat while they verified his alibi.

"I'll make some calls," Fox said.

Bradford nodded. They had to follow up. Although Coker was a bastard and dangerous, he didn't think he was their man.

"I'm going to check out that printout I got from CIRP," he said. "I think something in it may lead us to the truth." To the killer who was still free and on the streets.

And after Rosanna.

ROSANNA ALLOWED the security guard to escort her through the corridors to the elevator, but just as they were about to enter it, the fire alarm blared.

The guard's radio buzzed, and he snapped to answer it. "Yes, I'll be right there."

"What's going on?" Rosanna asked.

"There's been a disturbance upstairs and one of the offices is on fire."

"Which one?"

"I don't know. It's in the west wing, second floor. You'd better evacuate with everyone else."

People began to spill from the offices, elevator and staircase, and the guard raced toward the stairwell heading upstairs. She stood momentarily stunned, then it hit her that Dr. Klondike's office was in the west wing.

What if the man who'd tried to kill her the night before had come after the doctor now? What if Natalie and Terrance's death had something to do with the study, and more specifically *her?*

Guilt drove her to duck into the stairwell, and follow the guard. She pushed through two women who were panicked as they ran down the steps.

"You're going the wrong way," one of them shouted.

She ignored them and plunged on, determined to make sure the doctor was all right. Her breath caught as she exited the stairwell, and spotted the security guard chasing a man down the hall. Another guard laid on the floor near the doctor's doorway, unconscious, a bloody gash on his head. Smoke whirled into the hallway, spiraling toward the ceiling.

It was coming from Dr. Klondike's office.

Her heart racing, she rushed to the office doorway. Patches of flames darted through the room. Covering her hand with her mouth, she inched inside, searching for the doctor.

A second later, she spotted her body on the floor under her desk, her hair a tangled mess around her head. Rosanna dashed past the flames shooting up around the desk, leaned down and checked for a pulse.

But she didn't find one. God, no... The doctor wasn't breathing.

She had to save her, get her to a paramedic.

Wood hissed and the files on Dr. Klondike's office crackled as they caught ablaze. She shoved her hands under the woman's arms and began to drag her toward the door. But just as she reached it, another bout of flames burst up in front of her, blocking her exit.

BRADFORD had just settled down to study the information Dr. Klondike had given him when Captain Black poked his head in. "You aren't going to believe this, but there's a fire out at CIRP."

Bradford shot up from his chair, grabbed his weapon holster, shrugged it on and strode to the door. "I'm on my way."

He jogged to his car and started the engine, then sped toward Skidaway Island, questions gnawing at him. Was it possible that his visit to the research park had something to do with this fire?

And what about Rosanna? His heartbeat sped up, and he pressed the accelerator.

She'd said she had a session today—was she there now?

Chapter Fifteen

BRADFORD DIALED ROSANNA'S phone, then her shop, but she wasn't at either place. Honey, the girl who worked for her, claimed she'd gone to the research park.

Which meant she might be there now.

Fear clenched Bradford's chest as he barreled up to CIRP, jumped out and ran up the steps. Déjà vu struck him at the familiar scene. The fire alarm had sounded and people spilled onto the lawn, a chaotic mess of concerned and worried doctors and scientists.

A fire truck roared up and sprang into action, firefighters pulling on masks and running inside to check out the situation.

He jogged over to Dr. Hall. "What happened?"

"I don't know." The director looked

harried. "The security guard reported a disturbance on the second floor, west wing. Then someone smelled smoke and hit the alarm. I hope everyone got out all right."

So did Bradford.

Hall had no more information about the type of disturbance, then Bradford noticed a man wearing black clothing running around the back of the building.

"Police, stop!" he yelled.

Instantly alert when the man bolted, he ran across the lawn, dodging in between the mass of people to give chase.

The suspect fled into the marsh and for a minute, Bradford lost him. But then the brush parted, and he spotted a black shirt to the left, and pivoted in his direction.

Sea oats brushed his legs and shells crunched beneath his feet. He vaulted over a broken tree limb, closing the distance between him and the suspect. The man darted to the left and tried to make it to a small boat he'd tied to the inlet, but Bradford jumped him and knocked him to the dirt.

The man fought and cursed, but Bradford slammed his fist into his back. "Shut up and be still!"

Finally the man relented, and Bradford cuffed him, then dragged him to a standing position and hauled him back toward the front lawn. He was thirty-something, tall, fair headed, with soot staining his cheeks and the smell of lighter fluid on his clothing. "What's your name?"

The man glared at him with thin lips pressed together. "I want a lawyer."

The security guard approached, panting and heaving for air. "That's him, the man I saw on the second floor running from Dr. Klondike's office. It was on fire, and another guard was down. I think he's dead."

"Dr. Klondike?" Bradford's chest tightened, and he jerked the man by the arm, twisting it painfully. "Was she up there?"

He pinched his lips together. "I told you, I want a lawyer."

"Stay with him," Bradford ordered. "And when my backup officers arrive, put him in the squad car." Afraid the doctor and/or Rosanna might be in that office, he ran back toward the research hospital.

Knowing they'd stop him at the front door, he snuck past the firefighters through a side entrance. Smoke and the smell of burning wood assaulted him as he raced up the stairs. Then he did something he hadn't done in ages. He muttered a silent prayer that Rosanna was all right.

He had no idea why he cared so much, but he couldn't stand it if the killer had succeeded this time, and she was dead.

ROSANNA USED a blanket from the doctor's love seat to beat at the flames in the doorway, but they were jutting up too high, out of control. She could run through them and go for help, but she couldn't leave the doctor alone.

Desperate, she screamed for help and beat at the fire with more force, but flames rippled up the doorway and clawed at her feet. Finally they inched onto the rug in the office, and she ran back to the doctor and checked again to see if she was breathing.

Fear surged through her, but she'd heard the sirens roaring and knew the fire truck had arrived. Surely the firefighters would find them in time.

Frantic, she began CPR. Counting the compressions, alternately breathing into the doctor's mouth.

One…two…three…

Smoke hurled thicker and steady inside the room, and she swayed, dizzy, her own lungs filling with the plumes. She paused, gasped for air, shoved away her fear, then pumped her hands against the doctor's chest.

Darkness swirled in front of her. A welcoming abyss of nothingness. Free from pain. Nightmares. The choking smoke.

The infernal heat.

No…couldn't give in to it. Not now. Had to save the doctor.

She had to keep going. Another breath…

She swayed, felt the room spinning, pulling at her, the darkness beckoning. The fire heating her skin. Heard the sizzling of wood and paper, smelled the ashes.

She would be ash soon.

No…didn't want to die. Not yet. Hadn't finished her life. Hadn't found her destiny. Hadn't even been intimate with a man…

She wanted that intimacy with Bradford.

But her energy waned. Her arms felt so tired, her lungs unable to breathe. She fought fatigue, lowered her head and gave the doctor another breath.

Suddenly a gruff voice drifted to her above the noise of the fire.

"Rosanna!"

Bradford.

She glanced up, and stared through the flames. Saw him running toward her. A masked firefighter trailed on his heels.

Then water sprayed against the flames, they flickered and began to die. Bradford picked her up, but she pushed against him. "No, save the doctor…"

"Shh, she's breathing now. The rescue workers will take care of her," he said against her ear.

Lulled by the sound of his voice, by his comforting arms and words, she gave into exhaustion and burrowed against him. She was safe in his arms.

At least for now.

BRADFORD WAS SHAKING as he swept Rosanna into his arms. He thought he'd lost her this time.

Overcome with emotions, he had to clear his throat to speak. "Are you all right?"

She nodded. "What about the doctor?"

"The paramedics are taking care of her," he said.

The rescue workers continued CPR on Dr. Klondike, loaded her on a stretcher and raced down the steps. He carried Rosanna through the stairwell, then downstairs and outside into the fresh air. Another team of paramedics arrived, and he gently lowered her onto a stretcher in the ambulance. "Check her for smoke inhalation."

The EMT nodded, and Bradford leaned over, brushed her hair from her soot-stained face and told her he'd be back. By the time he reached the other ambulance, Dr. Hall was standing beside Dr. Klondike's prone body. But thankfully, she had been revived.

All because Rosanna had stayed with her and started CPR instead of saving herself.

The doctor looked weak, pale and was drawing in air through an oxygen mask.

"Dr. Klondike," he said gently, "can you tell me what happened?"

"Can't this wait?" Dr. Hall barked. "She's suffered enough. And her head is bleeding."

"I just need a minute." He squeezed the doctor's hand. "Were you attacked?"

She nodded.

"Did you see your assailant?"

She nodded again, then moved the oxygen mask slightly so he could hear her. "Warren Whitlock. He…saw you, didn't want his name released, anyone to know he was part of the experiment." She coughed violently. "Said bad press would ruin his political aspirations."

"Well, he's done that himself," Bradford said as Hall forced the mask back over her face.

He strode over to the squad car and spoke to the officer standing guard, then leaned against the side and addressed the perp, "Mr. Whitlock?"

The man jerked his head up and glared at Bradford, his nostrils flaring.

Bradford met his gaze with a cold expression. "That is your name, isn't it?"

"Yes," Whitlock muttered then reiterated his request for a lawyer.

Bradford gestured toward the young officer, Tomlinson, grateful Detective Fox had arrived with him and was canvassing the crowd, taking statements. "Read him his rights, take him in and book him, then fill Captain Black in," Bradford told Tomlinson. "I'll stop by and question him later."

The officer nodded and did as he was instructed. Then Bradford went back to confer with Fox.

"Have you found any witnesses?" Bradford asked.

Fox shook his head. "Stories are all the same. The alarm went off. They smelled smoke. Everyone panicked and ran out."

Bradford again relayed Dr. Klondike's statement, then pointed at Whitlock. "He started this fire."

"You think he's responsible for the other arson cases?" Fox asked.

Bradford pulled his hand down his chin. "I don't know. He lawyered up, but we'll push him at the station and make him talk. For now I'm going to check on Rosanna."

Fox's gaze turned wary. "Be careful with that one," he warned. "If she's part of a CIRP experiment, you may not be able to trust her. Sometimes they do things to participants that affect their minds."

Bradford knew Fox was talking from personal experience.

He also knew Rosanna was dangerous to him. The absolute wrong woman for him to get involved with.

But he was involved with her, he admitted silently. Much as he'd fought it, he wanted her with an intensity that was driving him insane.

"I'll get back to you," he said, then he wove through the crowd to the ambulance.

She looked frail and ashen-faced, but she was sitting up now, refusing the EMT's offer of oxygen. What an odd contrast of softness, vulnerability and courage she presented.

"I'm all right," she insisted. "I have to check on Dr. Klondike."

He collected her hands between his to calm her. "I talked to her. She's going to be all right." He lowered his voice. "We caught the guy who set the fire. Dr. Klondike said he didn't want his name released or anyone to know that he was involved in the research project."

Relief flooded her face, restoring some color to her cheeks. Around them, the sounds of curious doctors and scientists speculating over the cause of the fire rippled among the noise of the firefighters barking orders.

He addressed the paramedic. "Does she need to go to the hospital?"

The EMT shrugged. "Maybe for observation, but she refuses to allow us to take her in."

"I don't need medical care." Rosanna gave him an imploring look. "Please, I just need a shower and to get away from here."

"I'll take you home," he said quietly. "But later I have to go to the precinct to question our suspect."

"I don't have a home now," she said softly.

He squeezed her hands and helped her down from the stretcher. "I know. But I'll take you to mine." His heart pounded as he curved an arm around her and guided her back to his car.

Feeling a brief reprieve from the case now that he had a viable suspect under arrest, and confident it would take time for Whitlock's lawyer to arrive, he drove Rosanna back to Tybee.

She'd almost died again tonight.

As soon as they were alone, he had to hold her and remind them both that she was still alive.

ROSANNA COULDN'T shake the fear still gnawing at her nerves as she'd showered.

Thank God, the paramedics had revived Dr. Klondike and she hadn't died.

She'd also been terrified of dying herself. Afraid she might never get a chance to live out her life. To see Bradford Walsh again.

To make love to the man.

As the hot water pummeled her body, her skin tingled as if his hands were touching her, trailing over her sensitive nipples, down her back, over her spine, then lower and sinking into her.

Achy from the images bombarding her, she turned off the water, dried off and shrugged on the satin robe she'd bought earlier. The flimsy material felt cool and soft, rubbing against her in a way that made her feel feminine and desirable. And bold enough to hope that Bradford wanted her.

When she entered the living room, he was standing by the sliding glass door looking out at the backyard. It was growing dark outside, the gray clouds more ominous as the last vestiges of daylight waned. And even though it had rained the night before, the heat felt oppressive.

Bradford had showered and wore a pair of

jeans that hung low on his hips and a denim shirt that he hadn't bothered to button yet.

When he heard her approach, he pivoted, his masculine frame silhouetted in the shadows. He looked so powerful that hunger surged through her.

"Feel better?" His simple question seemed impersonal, but the husky timbre of his voice and the way his dark eyes slanted over her simmered with sexuality.

She nodded. "I still can't believe that man set Dr. Klondike's office on fire."

"Some people will go to any lengths to keep their secrets."

For a brief second, she thought he was talking about her, and she contemplated sharing the details of her past with him. But he would look at her differently if she did, and she wanted him to look at her with the same fiery passion that his eyes held now.

Even if that passion lasted for only one night. Even if he found out the truth about her later and hated her. The need, the ache, the hunger had to be quenched.

His dark eyes pierced her as she walked over to him, heady and filled with a quiet intensity that sent heat spiraling through her.

"You saved my life again," she said softly. "How can I thank you for that?"

"You don't owe me any thanks."

"I know." She forced a smile, desperately trying to read his expression. "You were just doing your job."

He hesitated, then cleared his throat, his voice arousing prickles of need along her spine. "Getting you out tonight was about more than me just doing my job."

His words fueled her hope, and she inched closer, so close she could see the fine dark beard stubble on his cheek. Her head swam with the scent of his masculine body as she moved closer.

"You should probably get some rest," he said quietly.

A smile twitched at her lips. "I don't need to rest."

He leaned toward her, feathered a stand of her hair from her cheek. "What do you need, Rosanna?"

She wet her lips, reached up and took his hand, then pressed it against the side of her face. "I need you, Bradford. I need you."

Chapter Sixteen

Bradford's restraint shattered like a twig in the wind.

He dragged Rosanna into his arms and kissed her thoroughly, his hands winding in her long red hair, the silky strands teasing the sensitive nerve endings of his fingertips. Fingertips that had never touched such softness. Fingertips that ached to trail over her naked body and into her warm, wet flesh. Fingertips that itched to give her pleasure, to make her moan his name as she flew apart in his arms.

She clung to him, and he deepened the kiss, driving his tongue into her mouth with a frenzy that made his heart pound. She tasted like exotic fruit, sweet and full of passion that burst to life and turned his body into a flaming inferno of need.

He backed her up, and they ended up against the wall, his body pressed into hers, his sex hardening and begging to be released from its imprisonment. She sank deeper into his arms, stroking his back and the taut muscles between his shoulder blades. Her fingernails dug into his skin through his shirt as he lowered his head and nipped and licked at her ear, the sensitive skin of her neck, then lower.

She had almost died tonight. A few minutes later, and she might have.

The thought of losing her triggered another round of frenzied kissing. He thrust his tongue in and out of her mouth, mimicking the way he wanted to pound his body inside hers. She tore at his shirt, and he wrestled free of it and threw it to the floor. Next came her robe, the unveiling of her naked body taking his breath away.

The gray light from the window painted shadows all across her supple curves, eliciting wicked fantasies of hidden desires.

"You're so beautiful," he whispered hoarsely.

She trembled beneath him, and he ran a hand over her face, then lower until he cupped her full breasts into his hands. She threw her head back with a ragged sigh, inviting him closer, coaxing him to touch her with her throaty cries.

He whispered her name, then flicked his tongue down her neck again, and traced a path over the curve of her breasts. She whimpered, and he captured one turgid nipple into his mouth and suckled her, bracing her with one hand as she swayed in his arms.

Pleasure rocketed through him as he fed on one breast, then the other, driven by the need to extinguish the fire in his body. A fire that she had brought to life, and one that could only be put out by her.

Need raging through him, he slid his fingers lower, traced them over her flat stomach to the mound of her femininity, then teased the insides of her thighs. She dropped her head forward this time, her hair brushing the side of his face as she planted soft, whispery kisses on his shoulder.

More kisses, made with low, suckling noises, drove him to tease her legs apart. She eagerly welcomed him, and he thrust two fingers deep in her, loving her with gentle strokes. Then he dropped to his knees and pressed his tongue over her wet nub of desire. Treating it to the same affectionate loving as he had her breasts, he pulled her tighter. Her breasts swayed as she moaned and trembled with excitement.

Seconds later, she cried out his name and flew apart, her body spasming and filling his mouth with a sweetness that made him want to grovel for more.

Unable to stand the wait any longer, he swept her up in his arms, and strode to the bedroom. She sighed, reaching for him, her eyes wild with hunger and passion, like a she-devil who had him under her spell.

His breathing erratic, he ripped off his jeans and socks, shucked his boxers, then grabbed a condom from his pocket. She watched, her face flushed, her arms urging him to hurry as she pulled him down to her.

He straddled her, wanting to look his fill, to feel her breasts again and her wetness, but she pushed his fingers from her legs as he trailed them over her stomach, then wrapped her fingers around his thick length.

A guttural sound tore through him, animal-like and primal. Then she wet her lips with her tongue and coached him to her center.

He slid between her thighs, stroked her with his hardness, felt the blood rushing to his head as he tried to hold back his climax. Taking one last look at the passion in her eyes, he claimed her mouth with his as he thrust inside her.

Then he heard a soft cry of pain and froze with sudden awareness. He'd thought she looked vulnerable, an angel in disguise, but he'd never dreamed she was a virgin.

ROSANNA WAS FLOATING somewhere between the clouds, the closest she would ever get to heaven without dying.

The thought of dying made her reach for Bradford. She wanted him to make her forget, to soothe her fears and give her more pleasure.

"Rosanna…" He started to pull away, but she clung to him, wrapped her hands around his hips and clenched him between her legs.

His hard, full length pulsed and throbbed inside her.

"Why didn't you say something?" he asked hoarsely.

"It doesn't matter."

"Yes, it does."

She shushed him by pressing a finger over his lips. "I know this is just for tonight. No commitments…" *That you couldn't love me.*

His dark gaze searched hers, troubled for a second, but the passion and hunger remained, so vibrant that she fell more deeply in love with him at that moment.

God, how could she be in love?

Her feelings didn't matter. The only thing that was important was this moment, his body slick and damp with perspiration, hot and hard from wanting her. Filling her with the most exquisite joy she'd ever experienced.

"Why me?" he asked in a gravelly voice that twisted her insides. It was even headier now because emotions echoed beneath the surface.

"Because I wanted you," she admitted with a sultry smile.

A slow grin tugged at his lips although his eyes still held worry, and doubt, reservations she refused to dwell on.

"Please…" She leaned up, teased his nipple with her finger, then her tongue, then dipped it lower, as she ground her hips against his.

He growled, then lowered his head and kissed her again as he thrust the rest of the way inside her. His thick, hard sex filled her, and she spread her legs wider, lifting her hips so he could bury himself more deeply in her.

Heat fired her cry of excitement, a riveting, soul-shattering primal lust that made her arch again and push against him. Her movements triggered his own, and they began to rock together, thrusting harder, deeper, faster, until the mind-numbing tingles that rippled along her nerves erupted into a hotbed of euphoria.

She spasmed and shivered against him as he thrust into her again, then he gripped her hips with his big hands and drove himself so far into her that he moaned as his body began to spill its release. She fell into a vortex of joy, a beautiful place of pure erotic sensations where she wanted to remain, lost forever in the mindless pleasure.

BRADFORD FELT completely humbled by the fact that Rosanna had given herself to him.

But why? He'd been suspicious of her, distrustful, had practically called her crazy.

Yet he'd wanted her anyway. He still did.

He buried his head against her neck, inhaled her essence and wanted to believe in the power of magic and love, but the grayness of doubt fell over him like a curtain closing.

Maybe he was the insane one.

He never should have slept with her.

"Stop thinking," she said softly. "I needed you tonight. It's as simple as that."

"Nothing about this is simple," he muttered. Still he didn't pull away or release her. He wasn't ready for that.

He rolled her sideways and cradled her in his arms, pressed her head into the crook of his shoulder and held her as if there might not be a tomorrow.

If he didn't find this killer, there wouldn't be.

Hopefully, though, the case was solved; he had Whitlock in custody.

Emboldened by that thought, he relaxed and sighed contentedly. A second later her lips tickled his chest. Her fingers traced a fiery path over his belly. Her whispered sigh told him that she wasn't ready to fall asleep yet, that she wanted more loving.

Bradford had never been a noble man. God knew that from the way he'd botched things with his family. He'd had his share of women and never committed.

And this one would be no different.

Still, as he lowered his mouth and tasted her again, he knew he had to have her one more time. And then maybe another.

For lurking in the darkest recesses of his mind, the idea that he might fail her and that the killer would get her, taunted him.

Fear surged through him, irrational and unwanted, but he channeled the emotion into passion.

Passion that urged him to take her into the shower, run his soapy hands over her naked slickness. To take her up against the wall with the water cascading over her breasts and his hands and mouth all over.

Then again in the bed with her on top, her beautiful creamy breasts swaying above him as he flicked his tongue over her nipples. Her glorious mane of hair spilled over his belly as she crawled beneath the sheets and went down under, giving him the best sex of his life.

The sweetness of their lovemaking on his

tongue as he took her with his mouth afterward obliterated any thoughts except that
her taste would linger with him forever.

ROSANNA MUST HAVE drifted asleep
because she dreamed of beautiful sunsets
and rainbows, that flowers danced around
her and that joy scented the air, mingling
with the fragrance of rain and wet sand,
and the sound of waves lapping gently at
the shore. In the dream, she was lying on
the beach beneath the sun, cozy and safe,
sated beyond imagination, nestled in the
arms of the man who loved her, the man
who was whispering her name as he kissed
her all over.

She slowly opened her eyes feeling
euphoric, but rolled to her side and found the
bed empty. Bradford's musky male scent
lingered on the pillow, which was still warm
from his head, yet a cold chill slithered
through her.

Where was he?

Shoving the hair from her face, she
slipped from the bed, found her robe and
pulled it on, then walked into the den. He
was standing in front of the open sliding

glass doors with his back to her, his arms by his sides, his hands knotted into fists. Naked, the sliver of light from the outside washed his skin in a golden-bronze color that made her body ache again.

But she saw his reflection in the glass, and her heart clenched. His mouth was set tight, and a haunted, tortured expression darkened his eyes.

He regretted their lovemaking. That was obvious.

Determined to prove that regrets were unnecessary, she moved up behind him, placed a hand on his shoulder. His muscles bunched, stressing the tension in his body.

She refused to let him push her away tonight. Not yet.

So she slid her arms around his waist, and leaned her head against his back.

"Bradford, what are you thinking?"

A sardonic chuckle split the air like wood cracking beneath the blade of an ax. "That I went way too far tonight."

"You only did what I asked," she whispered. "What I wanted."

He dropped his head forward. "That doesn't make it right."

"Shh. Don't worry. I don't expect anything from you."

"Don't you get it?" he growled. "You should expect something, a helluva lot more than an empty-hearted guy like me can offer." His body shuddered in her arms and she stroked her hands over his chest.

He stilled them with his hands. "You deserve a man who will make promises to you. A man who will take care of you and stay with you."

"I've been alone all my life, Bradford. I need a lover, not a caretaker."

"But you deserve one." He spun around, took a step away from her. "I'm not the man you think I am, Rosanna. I don't have an honorable bone in my body. I arrested my own little brother and sent him to jail. That's the kind of man I am, one who betrays his own family."

She swallowed hard, seeing the pain in his eyes, hearing it in his husky voice. "What did your brother do?"

He closed his eyes, inhaled, obviously struggling internally. "He was an arsonist."

His admission shocked her. Then she realized it made perfect sense—he understood this firestarter because his brother had been one.

"What happened, Bradford?"

"He started acting out when he was an adolescent. First setting fire to the grass. Some sticks. An old chair. Then an abandoned building. One day, the cat."

"Oh God…"

"His violence was escalating. I researched arsonists and knew he was in trouble. So I squealed on him, and he was sent to a juvenile home."

"You were trying to help him," she said softly.

"He sure as hell didn't see it that way. He hated me."

"Because he was troubled, and you gave him tough love," Rosanna said. "You had to teach him."

A self-deprecating chuckle rumbled from him. "That's what I told myself, but he thought I betrayed him. Even my mother tried to cover for him." He sighed. looking weary. "Then later he went too far. When he got out of juvy, he set fire to my bedroom. I put it out, but I knew he'd lost control. We had a big fight, and that night he burned down the juvenile home where he'd stayed."

"Was anyone hurt?"

A low sound of agony seeped through his gritted teeth. "Three kids died."

"You didn't betray your brother," she said softly. "He let *you* down. He was dangerous, and your mother was obviously living in denial." She closed the distance between them, cupped his face in her hands. "You are a man of honor, Bradford." *That's why I love you.* "You couldn't live with yourself if you'd let him kill someone else."

His dark gaze swung to hers as if no one else had ever understood his dilemma, how conflicted he'd been, how much he'd hated to lock up his own kid brother.

But she was right. He loved Johnny, but he couldn't allow him to hurt another person. The pain and guilt he'd lived with for years eased slightly.

A second later, he swept her into his arms and kissed her again, his touch hot with raw passion as he took her on the floor. She gave him what he needed, a wild, primal coupling that was frantic and hurried.

As he pounded himself inside her, and she

cried her release, she knew that leaving him would be the hardest thing she would ever have to do.

But she loved him too much to ask him to give something he couldn't, so she would let him go in the end.

BRADFORD'S BODY shook with the force of his release. He'd never get enough of Rosanna. Her soft, giving nature. Her luscious body.

Her whispered words of trust and acceptance.

He wanted her again and again, so much that it scared the hell out of him.

His cell phone trilled, slicing into his staggering thoughts, and he lifted his head from where it rested on her shoulder, aware now that he'd taken her on the braided rug on the floor and that she was still panting from his rough handling.

God, what had come over him?

The phone rang again. As much as he wanted to ignore it and cocoon them from the rest of the world, he was a cop; he had to get it. They'd arrested a man earlier for arson and attempted murder, and he had to question him.

He grabbed the phone and heard Captain Black's voice. "Whitlock's lawyer showed up. You want to be here when we question him?"

Hell, yes, he did. He wanted to kill the man for trying to hurt Rosanna. "I'll be right there."

Lifting himself off of her, he quickly explained about the call. He should take her with him, but she'd be safe here. No one knew he'd brought her to his cabin. And he had the alleged arsonist in custody...

Besides, he needed some space to get his head on straight. If Whitlock was their guy, he could close the case.

Then there would be no reason for him and Rosanna to see each other again.

HE STOOD OUTSIDE Bradford's house beneath one of the hundred-year-old oak trees in back, his blood heating as he watched Bradford take the woman on the floor.

So perfect Brad boy had finally tripped over that uncrossable line by bringing a person involved in a case into his own home. Even more interesting, from the looks of it, things had gotten real personal.

Laughter bubbled in his throat. Brad boy had just raised the stakes. He'd slap him on the back and congratulate him for being human if he didn't hate him so much.

Knowing Bradford had slept with the woman would make his revenge taste so much sweeter. He must care about her so he would feel even worse, guiltier, when she died.

And he should feel guilty, responsible.

Now Brad boy would suffer.

Smiling, he watched as Bradford left the house and drove away. Time to make his move.

He headed toward the sliding glass doors, itching to feel his hands on Rosanna.

Chapter Seventeen

Rosanna thought she heard the sliding glass door screech open, so she peered through the living room, wondering if Bradford had forgotten something. But the hulking silhouette of another man filled the doorway.

"Hello, Rosanna."

Her mouth went dry, and fear immobilized her at his ominous tone. He sounded familiar, almost like Bradford but different. Colder. Harder.

She fought panic. "How do you know my name?"

"I know everything about you." He took a step toward her, and she held up a warning hand, clutching her robe tightly together.

"I think you'd better leave."

A shake of his head caused his wavy hair to fall across one eye. She knew him—it was Kevin from the research project. "The party's just beginning, sweetheart."

A threat if she'd ever heard one.

She lunged toward the door to run, but he attacked her with a vicious yank, and twisted her arm behind her. The scent of smoke and sweat assailed her.

She fought against him, screamed and pivoted, then kicked at his knees. But he yanked her hair and slammed his fist into her face. Her head snapped backward, and darkness swirled like a tunnel clawing her down into its abyss.

She fought it, pushed at him, tried to scratch his face, his eyes, but another blow to her temple sent her flying backward into the wall. A scream died in her throat as she sank onto the floor in a puddle. The room spun, pain and nausea rocketing through her.

Cursing, he dragged her up by the hair, then hauled her into one of the kitchen chairs, positioning it in the middle of the living room. Desperate, she tried to break free, but he hit her again. She tasted blood and nearly passed out. His rancid breath brushed her neck as he tied her arms behind her back, and secured her feet to the chair.

A sob wrenched from her throat as he pulled her robe apart, then traced a finger over her bare shoulder.

His fingers were scorching hot and burned her skin as if he'd lit a match and touched it to her. Tears clogged her throat.

She was going to die tonight, then she'd never get to see Bradford again….

BRADFORD WRESTLED with pingponging emotions as he left Tybee and drove to the precinct.

He shouldn't have slept with a woman involved in his current investigation.

She had been an innocent. Had given him her virginity. He didn't deserve to be any woman's first.

Especially when he had nothing left inside him to give.

The best thing to do was to finish this interrogation, make certain they had their serial arsonist in custody. Then say goodbye to Rosanna.

So, why did that thought make his stomach knot?

Because he'd felt something shift inside his chest when he'd made love to her. And for the briefest of seconds, he'd imagined stupid things about love and having someone to come home to at night, things that no man like him had a right to even contemplate.

The sky looked ominous with gray clouds, and he wished it would rain and stifle the ungodly hot temperature as he parked at the precinct and strode inside.

Captain Black met him and they entered the interrogation room together. A stiff-necked, white-haired attorney with a bulbous nose introduced himself as Theo Palmer, while Whitlock sat with his hands clenched in his lap, his thick eyebrows pinched, his expression worried.

Captain Black slapped a file on the table. "All right. Let's talk, gentlemen."

The next few minutes dragged as they danced around the attorney's protests. "You have nothing on my client," Palmer said calmly.

"You're wrong." Bradford propped one hip on the table edge facing Whitlock. "Dr. Klondike survived and told us what happened."

Whitlock's face turned ashen, and he

leaned sideways to talk low into his attorney's ear.

Palmer folded his hands, appearing nonplussed. "What exactly did she tell you?"

Bradford narrowed his eyes at Whitlock. "That you attacked her and set her office on fire because you didn't want your name released as part of that research study." Any color remaining on Whitlock's face drained.

"But you were too late," Bradford snarled. "We already had a warrant and have that information, so you tried to commit murder for nothing."

Whitlock bowed his head into his hands. "My career on the City Council, my future in politics, it'll be over."

Palmer stared at them deadpan. "My client was assured that his part in this study would remain in the strictest of confidences or he never would have agreed to participate."

"We needed the name for an ongoing criminal investigation," Bradford said. "We didn't intend to print the list in the damn paper." He shoved the file forward, then opened it and removed the photos of the dead victims.

"Natalie Gorman. Hans Bolton, the waiter. Both of them in their twenties—both died in the bar fire at the Pink Martini."

Whitlock's eyebrows scrunched together as he stared at the morbid pictures.

"And this is Terrance Shaver. As you can see, he suffered—"

Whitlock waved away the pictures, his voice choked, "Why are you showing me this?"

"Because you just tried to kill Dr. Klondike by setting fire to her office."

Whitlock glanced at the pictures again and visibly shuddered.

"My patience is gone, Whitlock," Bradford growled. "We have a serial arsonist in the city, and three of his victims, now four, counting Dr. Klondike, were part of the CIRP research experiment. We found you tonight at the scene of the last fire—"

Whitlock shot up from his seat, his face contorted with fear and anger. "Listen, here, you can't pin all those fires on me."

"We know you set the fire tonight, that you didn't want anyone revealing who you were. Maybe these victims recognized you and you were afraid they would tell someone about your participation."

Whitlock pounded the table. "That's not true. I didn't even know that girl and those two guys. I certainly didn't set fire to those other places."

Palmer pressed a hand to his client's arm and tried to coax him to sit back down. "Mr. Whitlock, I advise you to calm down and let me handle things."

"But I didn't kill these people." His voice rose with agitation. "I'm not a serial arsonist. For God's sake, tonight was the first fire I've ever set, and I only did that because I was desperate." He paced across the room, a fine sheen of perspiration dotting his forehead. "I saw you there earlier asking questions and recognized you from the paper, so I got nervous. I went to talk to the doctor and asked her what you wanted and she admitted that she had released files on the paranormal studies. I tried to convince her to delete my name from the file, into telling you that it was a mistake that it was on that list, but she wouldn't listen. Then I lost my temper and pushed her." His voice cracked as he heaved for air. "She fell and hit her head—it was an accident. I never meant to kill her."

"But you set fire to her office and left her there to die."

"When I saw the blood I panicked…I didn't think anyone would believe me."

"So you decided to cover up her death with a fire?"

"Yes, I…guess I thought you'd blame that arsonist, that you wouldn't find me."

Captain Black made a sound of disgust. "You're a piece of work, Whitlock. You left an innocent woman to die, then you ran like a coward."

The man stopped in his tracks, stared at them both as if he'd just realized he'd confessed to attempted murder. Finally his face fell with acceptance and remorse.

"I'm sorry. I'm so sorry…" He collapsed into the chair, then dropped his head into his hands, his shoulders shaking.

Palmer spread his hands on the table. "Let's talk about a deal, gentlemen. My client has never been in trouble before. He told you the truth, that it was an accident—"

Bradford cut him off. "We're not talking a deal until we know about the other fires."

Whitlook looked so pale Bradford thought he was going to pass out. "I swear I had nothing to do with those," he said raggedly. "I'm not a murderer or an arsonist…"

Bradford studied his expression, the pitiful whine of his voice, and the regret in his expression.

Dammit. He wanted this to be the UNSUB. Wanted to lock him up and end this case and the reign of terror this fire-starter was wreaking on Savannah.

And on Rosanna.

But he believed Whitlock's confession.

His pulse clamored. God, Rosanna. He'd left her alone. And the killer was still out there. What if he'd somehow found Rosanna?

A JACKHAMMER was smashing Rosanna's skull.

No, it was the phone trilling. Slicing through the pain in her temple with its incessant shrill sound.

She blinked, trying to open her eyes, but reality swam back, and she closed them again, a sob wrenching from her.

Suddenly her attacker yanked her head

back, leaned over and whispered near her ear. "That's Brad boy. I'm going to pick up the phone, and you're going to talk to him."

She shook her head, but he pressed a finger to her breasts, and her skin sizzled with pain as if a match was burning her.

"You'll do exactly what I said," he muttered. "Or you'll suffer even more."

The phone jangled again, and he shoved it to her ear.

"Tell him I'm here then we'll wait on him to start the party."

Choking on the hatred bubbling in her soul, she glared at him, then cleared her throat, praying her voice worked. She wanted to warn Bradford, but how?

If she let him know this man was here, he'd be walking into a trap. Even if he saved her, he might die.

She couldn't bear to have another man's death on her conscious. Especially the man she loved.

"Are you ready?" he asked.

She nodded, sucking back another sob.

"Rosanna, are you all right?" Bradford's voice sounded strained. "What took you so long to answer?"

God, he sounded out of breath. Worried. Almost as if he cared what happened to her.

All the more reason she had to protect him.

"I'm fine. I…I just fell asleep."

"Thank God." He heaved a breath. "Listen. We finished questioning Whitlock, and he admitted to the fire at the research park, but not the others. I'm going to review that list I got from CIRP and see if I come up with anything."

Tears blurred Rosanna's vision. She bit down on her lower lip as her attacker ran his fingers along her neck, singeing her skin. "Okay. Bradford… thank you for the most wonderful night of my life."

Silence stretched across the line for a heartbeat, then he said in a husky voice, "I'll be there soon. Keep the door locked, and call me if you need me."

The phone clicked into silence, and Rosanna's hopes for a future shattered.

"You didn't tell him to hurry, that I was here," her attacker said with a menacing scowl.

She raised her chin defiantly. "I won't play your game."

He grabbed a kitchen knife, ripped off her robe and threw it on the floor at her feet and lit it. Then he pressed his hot finger to her breast and a fiery pain shot through her. "Sure you will. But we'll have to start the torturing before he gets here."

BRADFORD HUNG UP, anxiety bunching his muscles.

Rosanna's words echoed in his ears. She'd claimed she didn't want a commitment, but the emotions reverberating in her voice indicated otherwise.

He didn't want to hurt her. But he couldn't make promises…

"So what do you think about Whitlock?" Black asked.

Bradford rapped his knuckles on the desk. "I wish he was our UNSUB but I don't think he is."

Black sighed. "Yeah, I bought his story, too."

"Let me look at this list from CIRP," Bradford said. "Maybe something will stick out."

Black nodded. "I'll finish up with Whitlock and his lawyer."

Bradford scrubbed a hand over his beard stubble, the smell of Rosanna's skin lingering on his hand when he pulled it away. Ignoring the longing that made him want to ditch the paperwork, return to his cabin and take her back to bed, he began to skim the names.

To protect identities, the participants of the project had been assigned numbers, and the doctors had stipulated that in the group sessions, they use first names only.

Each participant had filled out forms detailing their health histories, along with questions on their personal backgrounds, jobs, relationships, likes and dislikes, hobbies and the special ability they professed to have, although the names hadn't been included on the forms, but rather their assigned numbers.

He studied the list of abilities, shaking his head as he found psychics listed several times, along with mediums and practicing witches. One participant stated that he or she dreamed the future, another floated outside her body through space and time, and ten people insisted they had telekinetic powers.

But one listing drew his eye. The person claimed to have the power to start fires with his hands.

He paused, remembering Rosanna's theory. The one he'd thought ridiculous.

There couldn't be any truth to this person's assertion.

Could there?

He flipped over to the profile and family history. The man who claimed to start fires had an unusually high body temperature. An odd magnetism to metal.

And he'd been struck by lightning as a child but he'd survived.

His pulse clamored. Rosanna had mentioned that she'd read about someone online claiming to be a firestarter who'd been electrocuted. And another struck by lightning.

He tensed, a ball of dread clenching his stomach.

His brother Johnny had been struck by lightning as a kid. But Johnny was in jail, in the hospital ward suffering from burns.

His heart pounded.

Although he hadn't actually seen his brother in the hospital, and he was severely burned and now bandaged...

Chapter Eighteen

Bradford checked the participant's number, then flipped through the files frantically searching for the person's name and contact information.

The initials JRW stood out in bold printed letters. His heart stuttered—they should have been emblazoned in red because they were his brother's initials.

The blood roared in his ears as he punched in the number for the Atlanta prison and asked to speak to the warden.

"Detective Walsh, I didn't expect to hear from you. I'm afraid your brother is still sedated—"

"Listen to me, is there any possibility that the man burned in the fire isn't my brother?"

"What? There's no way Johnny escaped. We haven't lost any prisoners."

But his face had been burned and bandaged. And he was sedated, so there was no way his own mother could have known that the man in the bed wasn't her son.

"How about transfers? Guards missing?"

A long pause. "Hold on."

Bradford heard the clicking of computer keys, then the warden hissed. "Actually we did have a guard who didn't show up the day after the fire. Called in and said he had to leave for a family emergency. He hasn't been back."

Hellfire and damnation. "The guy in the ward, can you check his fingerprints?"

Another sigh, filled with audible tension and the realization of what might have happened. "His fingers were burned, too."

"Go wake him up, have him verify his identity, then call me back." Bradford jumped up and ran for the door, punching in his home number as he ran toward his car.

If Johnny had escaped and had been here terrifying the people of Savannah, he'd done so to get revenge on *him*.

And if he'd targeted Rosanna, knew Bradford was protecting her and where he lived, she was in immediate danger.

Not that she hadn't been before, but Johnny would like nothing more than to hurt someone Bradford cared for.

And he did care for Rosanna.

God help him, he hadn't wanted to, but he did.

The phone rang once, twice, three times making his blood pressure soar. Finally someone answered.

"Rosanna?"

"No, bro, it's me."

His blood ran cold. He froze, one step away from his car, thunder rumbling above.

"Johnny, don't you dare hurt her, man—"

"Shut up, Brad boy. I'm in charge now. In fact, your girlfriend and I are here having a party. So come on over." A nasty chuckle rumbled over the line.

The insane ring to his brother's voice sharpened the terror streaking through Bradford.

"I didn't betray you, Johnny, and Rosanna has nothing to do with us."

Another laugh. "You screwed her, Brad boy, that tells me all I need to know. And come alone. If I see a hint of another cop, I'll light her up like a stick of dynamite and watch her explode."

Johnny paused, the silence driving home the reality of his threat. Bradford's throat thickened with emotion.

Johnny laughed, obviously realizing his taunt had upset Bradford. "And just think what her flaming red hair will look like charred and spread across the pillow her head rested on when you took her to bed earlier."

Rosanna's words rang in Bradford's ears, taking on a new meaning. She had been telling him goodbye because his brother had been there.

And because she knew she was going to die.

ROSANNA BIT her tongue to keep from crying out in fear as Johnny Walsh hung up the phone. Bradford's brother was a sick, twisted, sadistic animal.

No wonder Bradford had been forced to lock him up. He hadn't had a choice.

She couldn't help but compare him to Bradford. Even though he and this man shared the same genes, they were as different as night and day.

Just like her and her father.

Or were they?

She'd feared all her life that his rage lived within her. That that rage had given her the power to kill him.

She'd hoped she'd buried that rage so deeply beneath the surface that no storm could have unveiled it, but she felt it clawing its way upward, trying to surface.

But not for herself. For the injustice this man had done to Natalie and to the others. And to Bradford who still harbored guilt and hurt from the pain his brother had inflicted.

Bradford might not love her, but if she died, he would blame himself. Of that she was certain.

One reason she had to fight this monster. No matter what it took, she couldn't let him kill her.

She had to stall, keep him talking.

Maybe if she could concentrate, she could summon her power, if she had one, and untie her hands.

For the first time in her life, she prayed that she had that ability.

Johnny began to stalk her, circling her with sinister laughter, his dark eyes trailing over her as if he was envisioning her on fire, her skin burning beneath his fingertips.

Then he did burn her. With one touch his finger sizzled against her chest, creating a blister. She winced in pain, stifling a cry, unwilling to give him the satisfaction of admitting that he'd hurt her.

"Why are you doing this?" she asked between gritted teeth.

"Because my brother always thought he was better than me."

"He *is* better than you," she whispered. "He protects people instead of hurting them."

"He hurt *me*."

"No, *you* hurt others."

He stabbed her with another fiery finger, and she smelled the sensitive skin on her neck burning.

"Bradford doesn't hurt women," she whispered hoarsely. "He's a real man. He gives a woman pleasure."

Johnny leaned into her face, his rancid breath bathing her cheek. "He took you on the floor like an animal."

"He made love to me," she said quietly.

"Bradford doesn't know how to love." He

snagged her hair between his fingers, twisted it around his hand. His other one slid down to cup her breast, searing her with the heat from his finger again.

She spit in his face.

He reared back, anger flashing across his craggy features. He might be younger than Bradford, but he looked ten years older, weathered from prison.

Eyes wild with rage, he flicked out his hand and a ball of fire shot from his fingertips and dropped onto the floor, singeing the rug.

Rosanna shrank back from the flame, shocked to see his power in motion. Shadow hissed and lunged at him, but Johnny caught the cat and flung him across the room. She cried out, yelled at the cat to run. He screeched then disappeared into the bedroom just as Johnny dropped another fireball to her left. The fire popped and zipped toward her feet.

She closed her eyes, beckoning her own abilities, willing her mind to call upon its power. She tried to remember Dr. Klondike and Dr. Salvadore's instructions, tried to recall her grandmother's Native American stories about the strength of believing.

The rope jiggled slightly in her hands, and she desperately tried to shut out the noise of her attacker's breathing, the pain rocking through her, and the fire hissing around her as she focused on loosening the ropes so she could escape and save Bradford.

BRADFORD PARKED two blocks away from his cabin and went in on foot, his lungs tight as he slowly slipped through the shadows of the oaks backing up to his neighbor's property. He'd been in combat, had confronted the enemy without batting an eye, but nothing had ever terrified him as much as knowing that his brother held Rosanna captive, that her life rested in the hands of a coldhearted psychotic.

What was Johnny doing to her? Had he violated her? Was he torturing her with fire?

Had he killed her already?

His breath caught as he spotted his cabin. He'd half expected to find it already engulfed in flames.

But no, Johnny knew he was coming. Johnny knew he'd been with Rosanna and he wanted to drag this out, to make Bradford suffer.

He wove from tree to tree, the sound of the waves crashing in the distance mimicking the sound of his heart raging with fear.

Darkness bathed the house, thunder rumbling from the gray skies. He moved slowly, desperate to make his footsteps silent, watching the corners, searching the shadows in case his brother lay in waiting. Finally he inched his way up to the house, peered inside a side window.

Horror stabbed at him when he saw Rosanna naked, tied to a chair in the middle of the living room, with patches of flames encircling her.

Fury overpowered him, and he lost conscious thought for a moment. All he knew was that he had to kill Johnny and save Rosanna.

Then he'd never let anyone hurt her again.

He slipped around to the side of the house to the guest bedroom, then fiddled with the window until he opened it. Moving stealthily, he climbed through the window, his weapon drawn and ready. Something moved against his feet, and he realized it was Shadow. He knelt, stroked the cat, then gently put him outside to safety. "I'll save Rosanna, buddy," he whispered.

His brother's voice echoed from the front room. "Brad boy will be here soon. Then he'll know what it's like to suffer."

A whimper sounded from Rosanna, ripping at his gut.

Bradford tiptoed through the room, then hesitated at the doorway and checked his weapon. A second later, he inched into the door and braced his gun between his hands.

"Move away from her, Johnny, and I won't have to shoot you."

Johnny pivoted toward him, a leer on his face. He'd changed since Bradford had seen him. A scar grazed his left cheek and age lines crisscrossed his face. His scruffy hair and weathered skin made him look meaner than ever.

What little soul he'd once possessed was gone from his eyes. Instead they were wild, glazed, drugged from his thirst for vengeance.

A sneer curved Johnny's mouth. "I have my own weapon now, and you can't stop me." Johnny raised his hand and flung it toward Bradford. A ball of fire erupted from his fingertips and dropped at Bradford's feet, searing his boots as it exploded in front of him.

Bradford jumped back in shock. He hadn't seen a match. How had Johnny done that?

Another fireball popped and lit the floor in front of him, chewing the rug and filling the room with the scent of burning hemp. Then his brother's laughter boomed through the room, and Bradford jerked his eyes up toward him.

"What's going on, Johnny?"

"You thought you could stop me by locking me up, but I've only grown stronger over the years."

Rosanna gave him an imploring look as if begging him to leave her and save himself, though the flames flickering around her feet highlighted the fear in her eyes.

"How did you do it, Johnny? You learned some trick, found some nondetectable accelerant?"

Johnny shook his head, and lifted one hand, splaying his palms as if he were God. "I have power in my fingertips. I have ever since I was struck by lightning, but I didn't know how to utilize it until I read about the experiment at CIRP."

He turned to Rosanna. "She understands because she has power, too. Or at least she said she did."

"You were there in the study," Rosanna said. "You lied. You said you froze things with your hands. But Terrance Shaver read your real thoughts, didn't he?"

Johnny laughed again. "Yes, and he had to die."

Bradford stared at Johnny in disbelief, debating how to get to him and save Rosanna. She'd told him about the Web site... "You found out about the research study on the Internet, didn't you?"

Johnny nodded. "Once I escaped and showed the doctor my abilities, she signed me up immediately."

So Dr. Klondike had known that he could start fires, but hadn't spoken up. "How, Johnny?" he said, trying to buy time. "How can you do it?"

"Mind over matter," he said simply. "You know Mom was always afraid that when I was struck by lightning that it damaged me somehow. Instead it empowered me. Made me special."

Bradford remembered the doctor's reports from the study and from Johnny's childhood. Johnny always had an unusually high body temperature. Had sometimes shocked people when he touched them because of the electricity in his body.

And he'd been obsessed with fire after that lightning strike, had set fires in the kitchen, the woods, the backyard. Then he'd grown more conniving, had burned Bradford's personal belongings. Finally he'd turned his perversion on small animals...

But he could actually channel that heat into fireballs now without needing a match.

Bradford didn't want to believe him but he'd seen it now with his own eyes. And from Johnny's history, it somehow made scientific sense.

He glanced back at Rosanna, saw the flames jumping higher around her feet and clawing at her ankles. He had to act now.

"This fight is between the two of us, Johnny," he said quietly. "Let Rosanna leave and I'm all yours."

Johnny lifted his hand again and pointed it at Rosanna. "Put down the gun or she goes up."

"No, don't," Rosanna cried.

Bradford cocked the gun. "I said let her go, Johnny."

But Johnny reached over and pressed a

finger to Rosanna's neck. She winced in pain, and when his brother lifted his finger, a burn marked her neck. Several others dotted her chest and thighs, triggering fury to bolt through Bradford.

Rage ignited his blood as Bradford's gaze locked with Rosanna's. She was trying to be brave, trying to protect him.

He couldn't let Johnny hurt her anymore.

"I'm going to put the gun on the floor. Then let her go."

Johnny shrugged as if in agreement, but Bradford didn't trust him for a second.

Instead, he fired, sending a bullet toward his brother.

Chapter Nineteen

Johnny dodged the bullet, then threw another fireball at Bradford's feet, making him jump sideways to avoid it. Rosanna cried out in frustration.

Bradford didn't want to hurt his brother, but he was going to have to. Either that or Johnny would kill Bradford.

She couldn't let that happen.

Heat scalded her feet as the flames crawled toward her, growing higher. They had begun to spread, rippling across the braided rug between her and Bradford. Johnny stood in the middle, oblivious, as if the fire couldn't touch him.

Then Johnny tossed another ball of fire toward Bradford, so close it caught his pant leg ablaze. Bradford fired the gun again, but Johnny managed to avoid it, then Bradford beat out the spiking flames, but Johnny attacked him, and knocked the gun from his hand.

The next few minutes flashed by in a blur. Bradford and Johnny fought, trading blow for blow, rolling across the floor, through the fire, hitting and grunting like mad animals.

Johnny wrapped his hands around Bradford's throat and dragged him toward the flames so his hair was only inches from the blaze.

Rosanna had to so something. The ropes were loosening, and she wiggled her hands free. Smoke filled her lungs, and she blinked back tears as the thick plumes stung her eyes. She had to concentrate. Focus. Help Bradford.

Bradford managed to roll his brother over and pin his legs, but Johnny cursed and tried to knock him off. Forgetting about freeing her legs, she angled her attention toward Bradford's gun. Her heart pounding, she stared at it and poured all her concentration into making the weapon move. If she could slide it toward Bradford, he could save himself…

He would hate her afterward, would look at her differently, but at least he'd be alive.

The men twisted and rolled again, and Bradford shoved Johnny off for a second. But Johnny roared with rage and flung another fireball, this one catching Bradford's shirt. Bradford dropped to his stomach to extinguish the flames, and his brother lunged onto his back. The gun was only a few feet away.

She had to get it to Bradford.

Summoning her mental energy, she focused again, this time willing her power to surface. She'd moved that shelf to protect herself from her father. She could move that gun to save the man she loved.

Slowly the weapon began to slide toward Bradford.

Johnny slammed his fist into Bradford's lower back, but Bradford bucked upward, throwing Johnny off-kilter, then Bradford spotted the gun sliding toward him. He cut his eyes toward her, but she couldn't look at him. She needed all her attention on the weapon.

Another inch, another, and Bradford reached for the Glock. Johnny reared back like a wild animal, and pounced toward

Bradford, but he snagged the gun, spun around and fired. The bullet pierced Johnny's chest, blood splattering. Johnny shouted in disbelief, then his body bounced backward into the flames.

She cried out in horror as the fire began to eat at his hair and clothes. The flames were crawling up toward her ankles now, licking at her calves. Bradford jumped up to try to save his brother, but took one look at her, and ran toward her instead.

Heat singed her arms and stung her leg. As Bradford dived through the fire, beat at the flames, she quickly untied her feet. Then he lifted her in his arms and carried her through the blaze and out the front door.

"Where's Shadow?" she cried.

"He's safe. I let him outside earlier." As if the cat had heard his name, he loped up and rubbed against Bradford's feet.

Panting for a breath, he dropped to his knees, cradled her in his arms and rocked her while they watched the sizzling fire destroy his cabin and Johnny's body.

"I'm so sorry, so sorry," she whispered.

He pulled back and looked at her with narrowed eyes. "You moved that gun."

She nodded. "I had to…"

The stunned look in his eyes told her he couldn't accept what he'd seen, that he thought she was some kind of freak like her father had.

And that she was evil just like his brother.

BRADFORD CLENCHED Rosanna in a death grip as the blaze shot up into the sky, the past few minutes playing through his mind, imprinted there forever. He was still trying to make sense of what he'd seen…

He'd thought he'd die himself when he'd found Rosanna in the middle of that fire with his brother taunting her. And then Johnny had popped those flames from his hands and he'd gone into shock.

And Rosanna…she'd made that gun move toward him, but she hadn't been anywhere near it.

He'd never believed in anything paranormal but he'd just witnessed two instances in person. Yet she had lied to him, had never told him she had an ability.

In fact, when he'd specifically asked her, she'd claimed she didn't, that she'd joined the study to find out information for people at her store.

If she'd lied about that, what other secrets had she kept from him?

His mouth tightened and he carried her to his car, retrieved a blanket from the trunk and wrapped it around her. Then he grabbed a sweat suit he kept in the trunk and gave it to her.

"Put those on before the firefighters arrive."

She nodded, and he turned his back while she slipped them on. When he finally faced her again, acceptance warred with a feeling of betrayal. "How long have you been able to do move things with your mind?"

She chewed her bottom lip for a moment, then jutted up her chin, although wariness darkened her eyes. "Since I was four. It's called telekinesis."

Anger mounted inside him. He'd heard of telekinesis, just didn't think it actually existed.

"It's only happened once before," she said in a distant voice as if reliving some horror of her own. "The night my father died. He was drunk. He…came at me, was enraged, going to do God knows what. I was terrified, hiding in the corner and when he started to grab me, I made a bookcase fall on top of him."

No wonder she hadn't told the police.

"Since then, I've been scared to try to use my ability, afraid I'd hurt someone else," she continued. "I thought I was bad, that's what my father used to say." She sucked in a desperate breath, determined to spill everything. "The doctors at CIRP said I repressed my gift, but fear, emotions…well, the surge of adrenaline triggered my ability."

Like a person in a crisis who got an adrenaline rush and had superhuman strength. In a bizarre way, the explanation made sense.

The fire truck roared to a stop, along with two police cars. Firefighters and officers poured onto the scene. The next few minutes were chaotic and blurred as the paramedics examined Rosanna, and treated her burns.

Bradford relayed the events of the night to his captain.

Finally Detective Fox approached him. "I can take Miss Redhill to a hotel if you want."

"Thanks," Bradford agreed. "I have to make arrangements for Johnny's body."

Fox clapped him on the back. "You did

what you had to do, Walsh. Don't beat yourself up too much."

"I killed my brother. Now I have to tell my mother." Bradford clenched his jaw. "She hated me for putting him in jail. Think what this will do to her."

When he looked up, he saw Rosanna watching him. Knew she had overheard him.

But there was nothing left to say. She had lied to him, once again confirming that he couldn't trust anyone. And he had let emotions for her interfere with the investigation, and left her vulnerable and alone because he had feelings for her.

She had almost died because of him.

Now he'd closed the case, she could resume her life, would be safer without him in it.

There was no reason for him to see her again.

Resigned, he watched as the firefighters recovered his brother's charred body. He had to pay a visit to his mother and kill any lingering love she might have for him forever.

Rosanna knew Bradford was shutting her out. And she didn't expect him to forgive her or return her love.

But she refused to let him deliver the news to his mother about his brother by himself.

She pulled away from Detective Fox and gathered Shadow in her arms. "I want to go with Bradford."

He narrowed his eyes. "I don't think that's a good idea. Let me drive you to a hotel so you can clean up and get some rest."

She shook off his hand when he reached for her. "No. He's going to talk to his mother and I want her to know the truth. The whole truth. That she can't blame him for what happened tonight."

He stared at her for a long minute, then a small smile tilted his lip sideways and he took the cat from her. "He'll fight you on this."

She smiled in return. "I don't care. I have to do this for him."

A moment of silent understanding passed between them, then he nodded. "Good luck, Miss Redhill. You're going to need it."

She flattened her palms by her sides, then strode toward Bradford's car and settled into the front passenger seat. A few minutes later, he approached, a frown marring his handsome face when he saw her in the car.

"I thought Fox took you to a hotel," he said as he opened the car door and climbed into his seat.

"I'm going with you to see your mother."

He shot her an incredulous look. "The hell you are."

"You said she blamed you for your brother's arrest. Well, she's not going to blame you for his death."

"I killed him, Rosanna."

"Yes, to protect me. To give justice to Natalie and Terrance Shaver and that waiter." Her voice rose in conviction. "And to save all the other victims he would have murdered if he'd continued."

"I don't need you fighting my battles for me, Rosanna. Especially not with my mother."

She grabbed his arm and forced him to look at her. "I love you, dammit. And I won't let you do this alone."

Anguish darkened his eyes. "Rosanna—"

"I don't expect you to love me back. I know you think I'm evil like my father said, like your brother was."

He knotted his hands into fists, confused. "We all have good and bad in us, Rosanna.

But we make choices. You are nothing like my brother. You used your gift to protect yourself, to save me. Johnny used his to inflict pain and hurt others."

"But you had to kill him to save me," she said in a strangled whisper. "And I won't let you beat yourself up with guilt because you saved me. I won't let your mother—"

He cut her off, "Rosanna, you were a little child. For God's sake, you protected yourself the only way you knew how."

"Just like you did today, Bradford."

Anguish lined his face, and he closed his eyes and dropped his head forward, his shoulders shaking with grief. "My mother will never understand that."

"Then she's losing the best thing that she has in her life," Rosanna said softly.

Bradford opened his eyes, and something changed, softened in his features. "Don't you understand? You're better off, safer without me being around? My brother tried to kill you today to hurt me."

"But I'm alive and here, and you saved me." She pressed her hand to his cheek. "I'm just sorry your brother forced you to kill him. But that was his sickness."

His expression twisted with turmoil, then a low, throaty, tormented sound erupted from deep within him. "I'd do it again to protect you."

"I know," she whispered. "Because you're a good man."

"No. Because I hated him when he touched you. I couldn't stand to see him hurt you." His eyes welled with emotion. "I didn't care if he died, because I had to save you."

He choked, a terrible, anguished sound that broke her heart. Then he pulled her to him and his body shook with grief. She slid her arms around him, held him tight, felt his anguish inside her.

A few seconds later, he raised his head, looked into her eyes, and she saw love shining in the pain-filled depths.

"Rosanna…" His muscles bunched beneath her hands as he cradled her against his chest and kissed her. The kiss was full of turbulent emotions, passion, and the hunger that she'd felt the moment she'd laid eyes on him.

Finally he whispered the words she'd longed to hear all her life, the words she didn't think he would ever say. "I love you, Rosanna."

With a whispered sigh, he kissed her again, a tender kiss that made her heart swell with more love than she'd ever known existed.

And she knew that destiny had brought the two of them together.

Epilogue

Bradford hadn't wanted to believe in magic or paranormal powers or love.

But standing in the church, looking at Rosanna in that shimmery wedding gown and seeing the undeniable hunger and affection in her eyes, both directed at him, had changed his mind.

Their visit to his mother had gone as he'd expected. She'd been devastated to learn that her baby boy was dead. Shocked to see the photos of Johnny's latest victims. And somber when Rosanna had pleaded his case and showed her the burns Johnny had caused on her body.

But as they'd walked away, Rosanna had slipped her hand into his, and he had finally realized how much she loved him. She'd been so unselfish that she was willing to let his mother blame her for Johnny's death instead of Bradford. He'd known then that he was going to marry her.

Johnny had sealed his own coffin when he'd committed murder. Rosanna had helped him accept that fact and forgive himself, even if his mother couldn't.

In turn, he had helped Rosanna accept that she wasn't to blame for her father's death. Both her parents had abandoned her in their own way when they should have protected her. He also wanted her to know that she could use her ability around him; she didn't have to keep it a secret anymore.

He not only loved her, but he would also protect her with his life for as long as he lived.

The wedding march began, and Rosanna started down the aisle toward him, a bouquet of calla lillies in her hand, and he smiled, anxious to make her his wife.

Fall flowers scented the air, the crisp cool weather a welcome reprieve from the devastating heat of the summer. Sunlight streamed through the stained-glass windows, painting the church in various shades of muted colors.

His captain, Detective Fox and several of

the other officers lined the pews. Some of Rosanna's friends from her shop and two women she'd befriended in the research experiment occupied other rows.

Fox had managed to get Parker released from rehab for the day, and he sat in a wheelchair, still bandaged and struggling to recover, but alive and grateful Bradford had found the arsonist and solved the case.

Another person his brother had hurt and a reminder that Johnny had set his own collision course with death by starting those fires and murdering innocent people.

Although he'd hoped his mother might come, the front pew designated for family sat empty for both of them.

Then Rosanna mouthed that she loved him, and his heart swelled with emotions. From this day forward, they would be each other's family. Forever.

* * * * *

Rita Herron's popular
NIGHTHAWK ISLAND *series*
continues with UNDER HIS SKIN,
on sale in February 2008,
only from Harlequin Intrigue!

Turn the page for a sneak preview
of the first book in the new miniseries
DIAMONDS DOWN UNDER
from Silhouette Desire®,
VOWS & A VENGEFUL GROOM
by Bronwyn Jameson

Available January 2008

Silhouette Desire®
Always Powerful,
Passionate and Provocative

Kimberley Blackstone didn't notice the waiting horde of media until it was too late. Flashbulbs exploded around her like a New Year's light show. She skidded to a halt, so abruptly her trailing suitcase all but overtook her.

This had to be a case of mistaken identity. Surely. Kimberley hadn't been on the paparazzi hit list for close to a decade, not since she'd estranged herself from her billionaire father and his headline-hungry diamond business.

But no, it was *her* name they called. *Her* face was the focus of a swarm of lenses that circled her like avid hornets. Her heart started to pound with fear-fueled adrenaline.

What did they want?

What was going on?

With a rising sense of bewilderment she scanned the crowd for a clue, and her gaze fastened on a tall, leonine figure forcing his way to the front. A tall, familiar figure. Her head came up in stunned recognition, and their gazes collided across the sea of heads before the cameras erupted with another barrage of flashes, this time right in her exposed face.

Blinded by the flashbulbs—and by the shock of that momentary eye-meet—Kimberley didn't realize his intent until he'd forged his way to her side, possibly by the sheer strength of his personality. She felt his arm wrap around her shoulder, pulling her into the protective shelter of his body, allowing her no time to object. No chance to lift her hands to ward him off.

In the space of a hastily drawn breath, she found herself plastered knee-to-nose against six feet two inches of hard-bodied male.

Ric Perrini.

Her lover for ten torrid weeks, her husband for ten tumultuous days.

Her ex for ten tranquil years.

After all this time, he should not have felt so familiar but, oh dear, he did. She knew the scent of that body and its lean, muscular strength. She knew its heat and its slick power and every response it could draw from hers.

She also recognized the ease with which he'd taken control of the moment and the decisiveness of his deep voice when it rumbled close to her ear. "I have a car waiting outside. Is this your only luggage?"

Kimberley nodded. "I assume you will tell me," she said tightly, "what this welcome party is all about."

"Not while the welcome party is within earshot. No."

Barking a request for the cameramen to stand aside, Perrini took her hand and pulled her into step with his ground-eating stride. Kimberley let him, because he was right, damn his arrogant, Italian-suited hide. Despite the speed with which he whisked her across the airport terminal, she could almost feel the hot breath of the pursuing media on her back.

This was neither the time nor the place for

explanations. Inside his car, however, she would get answers.

Now that the initial shock had been blown away—by the haste of their retreat, by the heat of her gathering indignation, by the rush of adrenaline fired by Perrini's presence and the looming verbal battle—her brain was starting to tick over. This had to be her father's doing. And if it was a Howard Blackstone publicity ploy, then it had to be about Blackstone Diamonds, the company that ruled his life.

The knowledge made her chest tighten with a familiar ache of disillusionment.

She'd known her father would be flying in from Sydney for today's opening of the newest in his chain of exclusive, high-end jewelry boutiques. The opulent shopfront sat adjacent to the rival business where Kimberley worked. No coincidence, she thought bitterly, just as it was no coincidence that Ric Perrini was here in Auckland ushering her to his car.

Perrini was Howard Blackstone's right-hand man, second in command at Blackstone Diamonds, a legacy of his short-lived marriage to the boss's daughter. No doubt her father had sent him to fetch her; the question was *why?*

* * * * *

Get swept away down under with the glitz and glamour of the Blackstone empire as Kimberley tries to determine the real reason behind her "reunion" with Ric....

Look for VOWS & A VENGEFUL GROOM
by Bronwyn Jameson,
in stores January 2008.

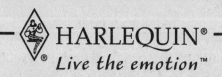

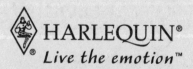

HARLEQUIN®

Super Romance®

...there's more to the story!

Superromance.
A *big* satisfying read about unforgettable
characters. Each month we offer *six* very different
stories that range from family drama to adventure
and mystery, from highly emotional stories to
romantic comedies—and much more! Stories
about people you'll believe in and care about.
Stories too compelling to put down....

Our authors are among today's *best* romance
writers. You'll find familiar names and talented
newcomers. Many of them are award winners—
and you'll see why!

If you want the biggest and best
in romance fiction, you'll get it
from Superromance!

Exciting, Emotional, Unexpected...

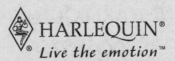

HARLEQUIN®
Live the emotion™

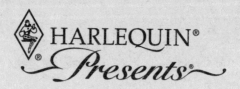

HARLEQUIN®
Presents

The world's bestselling romance series...
The series that brings you your favorite authors,
month after month:

Helen Bianchin...Emma Darcy
Lynne Graham...Penny Jordan
Miranda Lee...Sandra Marton
Anne Mather...Carole Mortimer
Susan Napier...Michelle Reid

and many more uniquely talented authors!

Wealthy, powerful, gorgeous men...
Women who have feelings just like your own...
The stories you love, set in exotic, glamorous locations...

HARLEQUIN®
Presents

Seduction and Passion Guaranteed!

HPDIR104

 **Harlequin® Historical**
Historical Romantic Adventure!

Imagine a time of chivalrous knights and unconventional ladies, roguish rakes and impetuous heiresses, rugged cowboys and spirited frontierswomen— these rich and vivid tales will capture your imagination!

Harlequin Historical . . . they're too good to miss!

SPECIAL EDITION™

Emotional, compelling stories that capture the intensity of living, loving and creating a family in today's world.

Modern, passionate reads that are powerful and provocative.

nocturne

Dramatic and sensual tales of paranormal romance.

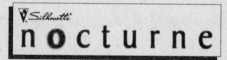

Romances that are sparked by danger and fueled by passion.